A FEAST OF DRAGONS

(BOOK #3 IN THE SORCERER'S RING)

MORGAN RICE

Books by Morgan Rice

THE SURVIVAL TRILOGY
ARENA ONE (BOOK #1)
ARENA TWO (BOOK #2)

the Vampire Legacy
resurrected (book #1)
craved (book #2)

the Vampire Journals
turned (book #1)

loved (book #2)

betrayed (book #3)

destined (book #4)

desired (book #5)

betrothed (book #6)

vowed (book #7)

found (book #8)

""Come not between the dragon and his wrath."

—William Shakespeare, *King Lear*

CHAPTER ONE

King McCloud charged down the slope, racing across the Highlands, into the MacGil's side of the Ring, hundreds of his men behind him, hanging on for dear life as his horse galloped down the mountain. He reached back, raised his whip, and brought it down hard on the horse's hide: his horse didn't need prodding, but he liked to whip it anyway. He enjoyed inflicting pain on animals.

McCloud nearly salivated as he took in the sight before him: an idyllic MacGil village, its men out in the fields, unarmed, its women home, tending linens on strings, barely dressed in the summer clime. House doors were open; chickens roamed freely; cauldrons already boiling with dinner. He thought of the damage he would do, the loot he would garner, the women he would ruin—and his smile broadened. He could almost taste the blood he was about to shed.

They charged and charged, their horses rumbling like thunder, spilling over the countryside, and finally, someone took notice: it was the village guard, a pathetic excuse for a soldier, a teenage boy, holding a spear, who stood and turned at the sound of their approach. McCloud got a good look at the white of his eyes, saw the fear and panic in his face;

in this sleepy outpost, this boy had probably never seen battle in his life. He was woefully unprepared.

McCloud wasted no time: he wanted the first kill, as he always had in battle. His men knew enough to give it to him. He wanted it so bad he could taste it.

McCloud whipped his horse again, until it shrieked, and gained speed, heading out farther in front of the others. He raised his ancestor's spear, a heavy thing of iron, leaned back, and hurled it.

As always, his aim was true: the boy had barely finished turning when the spear met his back, sailing right through it and pinning him to a tree with a whooshing noise. Blood gushed from his back, and it was enough to make McCloud's day.

McCloud let out a short cry of joy as they all continued charging, across the choice land of the MacGils, through yellow cornstalks swaying in the wind, up to his horse's thighs, and towards the village gate. It was almost too beautiful a day, too beautiful a picture, for the devastation that they were about to enact.

They charged through the unprotected gate of the village, this place dumb enough to be situated on the outskirts of the Ring, so close to the Highlands. They should have known better, McCloud thought with scorn, as he swung an axe and chopped down the wooden sign announcing the place. He would rename it soon enough.

His men entered the place, and all around him screams erupted of women, of children, of old men, of whomever happened to be home in this godforsaken place. There were probably a hundred unlucky souls, and McCloud was determined to make each one of them pay. He raised his axe high overhead as he focused on one woman in particular, running with her back to him, trying for dear life to make it back to the safety of her home. It was not meant to be.

McCloud's axe hit her in the back of her calf, as he had wanted, and she went down with a shriek. He hadn't wanted to kill her: only to maim her. After all, he wanted her alive for the pleasure he would have with her afterwards. He had chosen her well: a woman with long, untamed blond hair and narrow hips, hardly over eighteen. She would be his. And when he was done with her, perhaps he would kill her then. Or perhaps not; perhaps he would keep her as his slave.

He screamed in delight as he rode up next to her and jumped off his horse in mid-stride, landing on top of her and tackling her to the ground. He rolled with her on the dirt, feeling the impact of the road, and smiled as he relished what it felt like to be alive.

Finally, life had meaning again.

CHAPTER TWO

Kendrick stood in the eye of the storm, in the Hall of Arms, flanked by dozens of his brothers, all hardened members of the Silver, and looked calmly back at Darloc, the commander of the royal guard sent on an unfortunate mission. What had Darloc been thinking? Did he really think he could march into the Hall of Arms and try to arrest Kendrick, the most loved of the royal family, in front of all his brothers in arms? Did he really think the others would stand by and allow it?

He had vastly underestimated The Silver's loyalty to Kendrick. Even if Darloc had arrived with legitimate charges for his arrest—and these certainly were not—Kendrick doubted very much that his brothers would allow him to be carted away. They were loyal for life, and loyal to the death. That was the creed of The Silver. He would have reacted the same way if any of his brethren were threatened. After all, they had all trained together, fought together, for all their lives.

Kendrick could feel the tension that hung in the thick silence, as The Silver held their weapons drawn at the mere dozen royal guards, who shifted where they stood, looking more uncomfortable by the moment. They must have known it would be a massacre if any of them tried for their swords—and wisely, none did. They all stood there and awaited the order of their commander, Darloc.

Darloc swallowed, looking very nervous. He realized his cause was hopeless.

"It seems you have not come with enough men," Kendrick responded calmly, smiling. "A dozen of the King's Guard against a hundred of The Silver. Yours is a lost cause."

Darloc flushed, looking very pale. He cleared his throat.

"My liege, we all serve the same kingdom. I do not wish to fight you. You are correct: this is a fight we could not win. If you command us, we will leave this place and return to the King.

But you know that Gareth would just send more men for you. Different men. And you know where this will all lead. You might kill them all—but do you really want the blood of your fellow brothers on your hands? Do you really want to spark a civil war? For you, your men would risk their lives, kill anyone. But is that fair to them?"

Kendrick stared back, thinking it all through. Darloc had a point. He did not want any of his men hurt solely on his account. He felt an overwhelming desire to protect them from any bloodshed, no matter what that meant for him. And however awful his brother Gareth was, and however bad a ruler, he did not want a civil war—at least, not on his account. There were other ways; direct confrontation, he had learned, was most often the least effective.

Kendrick reached over and slowly lowered his friend Atme's sword. He turned and faced the other Silver. He was overwhelmed with gratitude to them for coming to his defense.

"My fellow Silver," he announced. "I am humbled by your defense, and I assure you it is not in vain. As you all know me, I had nothing to do with the death of my father, our former king. And when I find his true killer, whom I suspect I have already found from the nature of these orders, I shall be the first to have vengeance. I stand falsely accused. That said, I do not wish to be the impetus for a civil war. So please, lower your arms. I will allow them to take me peacefully. For one member of the Ring should never fight another. If justice lives, then the truth will come out—and I will be returned to you promptly."

The group of Silver slowly, reluctantly, lowered their arms as Kendrick turned back to Darloc. Kendrick stepped forward and walked with Darloc for the door, the King's Guard surrounding him. Kendrick walked proudly, in the center, erect. Darloc did not try to shackle him—perhaps out of respect, or out of fear, or because Darloc knew he was innocent. Kendrick would lead himself to his new prison. But he would not give in so easily. Somehow he would clear his name, get himself freed from the dungeon—and kill his father's murderer. Even if it was his own brother.

CHAPTER THREE

Gwendolyn stood in the bowels of the castle, her brother Godfrey beside her, and stared back at Steffen as he stood there, shifting, twisting his hands. He was an odd character—not just because he was deformed, his back twisted and hunched, but also because he seemed to be filled with a nervous energy. His eyes never stopped shifting, and his hands clasped each other as if he were wracked with guilt. He rocked in place as he stood, shifting from foot to foot, and hummed to himself in a deep voice. All these years of being down here, Gwen figured, all these years of isolation had clearly forged him into an odd character.

Gwen waited in anticipation for him to finally open up, to reveal what had happened to her father. But as seconds turned into minutes, as the sweat increased on Steffen's brow, as he rocked ever more dramatically, nothing came. There continued to be just a thick, heavy silence, punctuated only by his humming noises.

Gwen was beginning to sweat herself down here, the roaring fires from the pits too close on this summer day. She wanted to be finished with this, to leave this place—and never return here again. She scrutinized Steffen, trying to decipher his expression, to figure out what ran through his mind. He had promised to tell them something, but now he had fallen silent. As she examined him, it appeared he was having second thoughts. Clearly, he was afraid; he had something to hide.

Finally, Steffen cleared his throat.

"Something fell down the chute that night, I admit it," he began, not making eye contact, looking somewhere on the floor, "but I'm not sure what it was. It was metal. We took the chamber pot out that night, and I heard something land in the river. Something different. So," he said, clearing his throat several times as he wrung his hands, "you see, whatever it is, it washed away, in the tides."

"Are you certain?" Godfrey demanded.

Steffen nodded vigorously.

Gwen and Godfrey exchanged a look.

"Did you get a look at it, at least?" Godfrey pressed.

Steffen shook his head.

"But you made mention of a dagger. How did you know it was a dagger if you did not see it?" Gwen asked. She felt certain that he was lying; she just did not know why.

Steffen cleared his throat.

"I said so because I just assumed it was a dagger," he responded. "It was small and metal. What else could it be?"

"But did you check the bottom of the pot?" Godfrey asked. "After you dumped it? Maybe it is still in the pot, at the bottom."

Steffen shook his head.

"I checked the bottom," he said. "I always do. There was nothing. Empty. Whatever it was, it was washed away. I saw it float away."

"If it was metal, how did it float?" Gwen asked.

Steffen cleared his throat, then shrugged.

"The river is mysterious," he answered. "Tides are strong."

Gwen exchanged a skeptical look with Godfrey, and she could tell from his expression that he did not believe Steffen, either.

Gwen was growing increasingly impatient. Now, she was also baffled. It had seemed just moments before that Steffen was going to tell them everything, as he had promised. But it seemed as if he had suddenly changed his mind.

Gwen took a step closer to him and scowled, sensing that this man had something to hide. She put on her toughest face, and as she did, she felt the strength of her father pouring through her. She was determined to discover whatever it was he knew— especially if it would help her find her father's killer.

"You are lying," she said, her voice steely cold, the strength in it surprising even her. "Do you know what the punishment is for lying to a member of the royal family?"

Steffen wrung his hands and nearly bounced in place, glancing up at her for a moment, then quickly looking away.

"I'm sorry," he said. "I'm sorry. Please, I have nothing more."

"You asked us before if you would be spared from jail if you told us what you knew," she said. "But you have told us nothing. Why would you ask that question if you had nothing to tell us?"

Steffen licked his lips, looking down at the floor.

"I... I...um," he started and stopped. He cleared his throat. "I was worried...that I would get in trouble for not reporting that an object came down the chute. That is all. I am sorry. I do not know what it was. It's gone."

Gwen narrowed her eyes, staring at him, trying to get to the bottom of this strange character.

"What happened to your master, exactly?" she asked, not letting him off the hook. "We are told he went missing. And that you had something to do with it."

Steffen shook his head again and again.

"He left," Steffen answered. "That is all I know. I'm sorry. I know nothing that can help you."

Suddenly there came a loud swooshing noise from across the room, and they all turned to see waste come flying down the chute, and land with a splat in the huge chamber pot. Steffen turned and ran across the room, hurrying over to the pot. He stood beside it, watching as it filled with waste from the upper chambers.

Gwen turned and looked at Godfrey, who stared back at her. He wore an equally baffled expression.

"Whatever he's hiding," she said, "he won't give it up."

"We could have him imprisoned," Godfrey said. "That might get him to speak."

Gwen shook her head.

"I don't think so. Not with this one. He's obviously extremely afraid. I think it has to do with his master. He's clearly torn about something, and I don't think it has to do with father's death. I think he knows something that might help us—but I sense that cornering him will only make him shut down."

"So what should we do?" Godfrey asked.

Gwen stood there, thinking. She remembered a friend of hers, when she was young, who had once been caught lying. She remembered her parents had pressured her every which way to tell the truth, but she would not. It was only weeks later, when everyone had finally left her alone, that she had stepped forward voluntarily and revealed everything. Gwen sensed the same energy coming off of Steffen, that backing him into a corner would make him shut down, that he needed space to come forward on his own.

"Let's give him time," she said. "Let's search elsewhere. Let's see what we can find out, and circle back to him when we have more. I think he'll open up. He's just not ready."

Gwen turned and watched him, across the room, examining the waste as it filled the cauldron. She felt certain that he would lead them to her father's murderer. She just did not know how. She wondered what secrets lurked in the depths of his mind.

He was a very strange character, Gwen thought. Very strange, indeed.

CHAPTER FOUR

Thor tried to breathe as he blinked back the water which covered his eyes, his nose, his mouth, pouring down all around him. After sliding across the boat, he had finally managed to grab hold of the wooden railing, and he clung to it for dear life as the relentless water worked away at his grip. Every muscle in his body was shaking, and he did not know how much longer he could hold on.

All around him his brothers did the same, clinging to dear life for whatever they could find as the water tried to drive them off the boat. Somehow, they held on.

The sound was deafening, and it was hard to see more than a few feet in front of him. Despite the summer day the rain was cold, and the water sent a chill through his body he could not shake. Kolk stood there, scowling, hands on his hips as if impervious to the rain wall, and barked out all around him.

"GET BACK TO YOUR SEATS!" he screamed. "ROW!"

Kolk himself took a seat and began rowing, and within moments the boys slipped and crawled across the deck, heading back for the benches. Thor's heart pounded as he let go himself, and struggled to cross the deck. Krohn, inside his shirt, whined, as Thor slipped then fell, landing hard on the deck.

He crawled the rest of the way, and soon found himself back in his seat.

"TIE YOURSELF IN!" Kolk screamed.

Thor looked down and saw the knotty ropes beneath his bench, and finally realized what they were for: he reached down and tied one around his wrist, chaining himself to the bench and the oar.

It worked. He stopped slipping. And soon, he was able to row.

All around him the boys resumed their rowing, Reese taking a seat in front of him, and Thor could feel the boat moving. Within minutes, the rain wall lightened up ahead.

As he rowed and rowed, his skin burning from this strange rain, every muscle in his body aching, finally the sound of the rain began to subside, and Thor began to feel less water pouring down on his head. In a few more moments, they entered a sunny sky.

Thor looked about, shocked: it was completely dry, bright. It was the strangest thing he had ever experienced: half the boat was under a dry, shining sun, while the other half was being poured on as they passed through the rain wall.

Finally, the entire boat was under a clear blue and yellow sky, the warm sun beating down on them. It was silent now, the rain wall disappearing fast, and all of his brothers in arms looked at each other, stunned. It was as if they had passed through a curtain, to another realm.

"YIELD!" yelled Kolk.

All around Thor boys dropped their oars with a collective groan, gasping, catching their breath. Thor did the same, feeling every muscle in his body trembling and so grateful to have a break. He slumped over, gasped for air and tried to relax his aching muscles as their boat glided into these new waters.

Thor finally regained himself and stood and looked around. He looked down at the water, and saw that it had changed color: it was now a light, glowing red. They had entered a different sea.

"The Sea of Dragons," Reese said, beside him, also looking down in wonder. "They say it runs red with the blood of its victims."

Thor looked down at it. It bubbled in places, and in the distance strange beasts surfaced from the water momentarily, then submerged. None lingered long enough for him to get a good look at them, but he did not want to try his luck and lean down any closer.

Thor turned and took it all in, disoriented. Everything here, on this side of the rain wall, seemed so foreign, so different. There was even a slight red mist in the air, hovering low over the water. He surveyed the horizon and spotted dozens of small islands, spread out, like stepping stones on the horizon.

A strong breeze picked up and Kolk stepped forward and barked:

"RAISE THE SAILS!"

Thor jumped into action with all the boys around him, grabbing the ropes, and hoisting them to catch the breeze. The sails caught and a gust of wind carried them. Thor felt the boat moving beneath them faster than it ever had, and they aimed for the islands. The boat rocked on huge, rolling waves, which rose up out of nowhere, gently moving up and down.

Thor made his way towards the bow, leaned against the rail and looked out. Reese came up beside him, and O'Connor came up on his other side. They all stood side-by-side, and Thor watched as the chain of islands fast approached. They stood there in silence for a long time, Thor relishing the moist breezes as his body relaxed.

Finally, Thor realized they aimed for one island in particular. It grew larger, and Thor felt a chill as he realized it was their destination.

"The Isle of Mist," Reese said, in awe.

Thor studied it in wonder. Its shape began to come into focus—it was rocky and craggy, barren, and it stretched several miles in each direction, long and narrow, shaped like a horseshoe. Huge waves crash against its shore, rumbling even from here, creating huge sprays of foam as they met enormous boulders. There was the tiniest strip of land beyond the boulders, and then a wall of cliffs which soared straight up, high into the air. Thor did not see how their boat could safely land.

Adding to the strangeness of this place, a red mist lingered all over the island, like a dew, sparkling in the sun. It gave it an ominous feel. Thor could sense something inhuman, unearthly, about this place.

"They say it's survived millions of years," O'Connor added. "It's older than the Ring. Older, even, than the Empire."

"It belongs to the dragons," Elden added, coming up beside Reese.

As Thor watched, suddenly the second sun plummeted in the sky; in moments the day went from sunny and bright to nearly sunset, the sky tainted with reds and purples. He could not believe it: he had never seen the sun move that quickly before. He wondered what else was different in this part of the world.

"Does a dragon live on this isle?" Thor asked.

Elden shook his head.

"No. I hear it lives close by. They say that red mist is forged from a dragon's breath. He breathes at night on a neighboring island, and the wind carries it and covers the island by day."

Thor heard a sudden noise; at first it sounded like a low rumble, like thunder, long and loud enough to shake the boat. Krohn, still in his shirt, ducked his head and whined.

The others all spun and Thor turned too and looked out; somewhere on the horizon he thought he could see the faint outline of flames licking the sunset, then disappearing in black smoke, like a small volcano erupting.

"The Dragon," Reese said. "We are in its territory now."

Thor swallowed, wondering.

"But then how can we be safe here?" O'Connor asked.

"You're not safe anywhere," came a resounding voice.

Thor spun to see Kolk standing there, hands on his hips, watching the horizon over their shoulders.

17

"That is the point of The Hundred, to live with the risk of death each day. This is not an exercise. The dragon lives close, and there's nothing to stop him from attacking. He likely will not, because he jealously guards his treasure on his own isle, and dragons don't like to leave treasure unprotected. But you will hear his roars, and see his flames at night. And if we anger him somehow, there's no telling what could happen."

Thor heard another low rumble, saw another burst of flame on the horizon, and watched as they got closer and closer to the isle, waves crashing against it. He looked up at the steep cliffs, a wall of rock, and wondered how they would ever get up to the top, to its flat and dry land.

"But I see nowhere for a ship to dock," Thor said.

"That would be too easy," Kolk shot back.

"Then how do we get onto the island?" O'Connor asked.

Kolk smiled down, an evil smile.

"You swim," he said.

For a moment, Thor wondered if he was kidding; but then he realized from the look on his face that he was not. Thor swallowed.

"Swim?" Reese echoed, unbelieving.

"Those waters are teaming with creatures!" Elden said.

"Oh, that's the least of it," Kolk continued. "Those tides are treacherous; those whirlpools will suck you down; those waves will smash you into those jagged rocks; the water is hot; and if you make it past the rocks, you'll have to find a way to climb those cliffs, to reach dry land. If the sea creatures don't get you first. Welcome to your new home."

Thor stood there with the others, at the rail's edge, looking down at the foaming sea beneath him. The water swirled beneath him like a living thing, the tides growing stronger by the second, rocking the boat, making it harder to keep his balance. Down below, the waters raged, churning, a bright red which seemed to contain the blood of hell itself. Worse of all, as Thor watched closely, these waters were disturbed every few feet by the surfacing of another sea monster, rising up, snapping its long teeth, then submerging.

Their ship suddenly dropped anchor, so far from shore, and Thor swallowed. He looked up at the boulders framing the island, and wondered how they would make it from here to there. The crashing of the waves grew louder by the second, making others have to shout to be heard.

As he watched, several small rowboats were lowered into the water, then guided by the commanders far from the ship, a good thirty yards. They would not make it that easy: they would have to swim to reach them.

The thought of it made Thor's stomach turn.

"JUMP!" Kolk screamed.

For the first time, Thor felt afraid. He wondered if that made him less of a Legion member, less of a warrior. He knew that warriors should be fearless at all times. But he had to admit to himself that he felt fear now. He hated the fact that he did, and he wished it could be otherwise. But he did.

But as Thor looked around and saw the terrified faces of the other boys, he felt better. All around him boys stood close to the rail, frozen in fear, staring down at the waters. One boy in particular was so scared that he shook. It was the boy from the day of the shields, the one who had been afraid, who had been forced to run laps.

Kolk must have sensed it, because he crossed the boat towards him. Kolk seemed unaffected as the wind threw back his hair, grimacing as he went, looking ready to conquer nature itself. He came up beside him and his scowl deepened.

"JUMP!" Kolk screamed.

"No!" the boy answered. "I can't! I won't do it! I can't swim! Take me back home!"

Kolk walked right up to the boy, as he was beginning to back away from the rail, grabbed him by the back of his shirt, and hoisted him high off the ground.

"Then you shall learn to swim!" Kolk snarled, and then, to Thor's disbelief, he hurled the boy over the edge.

The boy went flying through the air, screaming, as he plummeted a good fifteen feet towards the foaming sea. He landed with a splash, then floated to the surface, flailing, gasping for air.

"HELP!" he screamed.

"What's the first law of the Legion?" Kolk screamed out, turning to the other boys on ship, ignoring the boy in the water.

Thor was dimly aware of the correct response, but was too distracted by the sight of the boy, drowning below, to answer.

"To help a fellow Legion member in need!" Elden screamed out.

"And is he in need?" Kolk yelled, pointing down to the boy.

The boy raised his arms, bobbing in and out of the water, and the other boys stood on deck, staring, all too scared to dive in.

At that moment, something funny happened to Thor. As he focused on the drowning boy, everything else fell away. Thor no longer thought of himself. The fact that he might die never even entered his mind. The sea, the monsters, the tides...it all faded away. All he could think of was rescuing someone else.

Thor stepped up onto the wide, oak rail, bent his knees, and without thinking, leapt high into the air, heading face first for the bubbling red of the waters beneath him.

CHAPTER FIVE

Gareth sat on his father's throne in the Grand Hall, rubbing his hands along its smooth, wooden arms and looking out at the scene before him: thousands of his subjects were packed into the room, people flocking in from all corners of The Ring to watch this once-in-a-lifetime event, to see if he could wield the Dynasty Sword. To see if he was the Chosen One. Not since his father was young had the people had a chance to witness a hoisting— and no one seemed to want to miss it. Excitement hung in the air like a cloud.

Gareth himself was numb with anticipation. As he watched the room continue to swell, more and more people packed inside, he started to wonder whether his father's advisors has been right, whether indeed it had been a bad idea to hold the hoisting in the Grand Hall and to open it to the public. They had urged him to attempt it in the small, private Sword Chamber; they had reasoned that if he failed, few would witness it. But Gareth did not trust his father's people; he felt more confident in his destiny than his father's old guard, and he wanted the entire kingdom to witness his accomplishment, to witness that he was the Chosen One, as it happened. He had wanted the moment recorded in time. The moment his destiny had arrived.

Gareth had entered the room with a flair, had strutted through accompanied by his advisors, wearing his crown and mantle, wielding his scepter—he wanted them all to know that he, not his father, was the true King, the true MacGil. It had not taken him as long as he had expected to feel that this was his castle, these his subjects. He wanted his people to feel it now, this show of power to be widely seen. After today, they would know for certain that he was there one and only true king.

But now that Gareth sat there, alone on the throne, looking out at the vacant iron prongs in the center of the room in which the sword would be placed, lit up by a shaft of sunlight pouring down through the ceiling, he was not so sure. The gravity of what he was about to do weighed down on him; it would be an irreversible step, and there was no turning back. What if, indeed, he failed? He tried to push it from his mind.

The huge door opened with a creak on the far side of the room, and with an excited hush, the room fell silent in anticipation. In marched a dozen of the court's strongest hands, holding the sword between them, all struggling under its weight. Six men stood on each side, and they noticeably struggled under its weight. They marched slowly, one step at a time, carrying the sword towards the vacant prongs in the center of the room.

Gareth's heart quickened as he watched it get closer. For a brief moment, his confidence wavered—if these twelve men, larger than any he had ever seen, could barely hold it, what chance was there for him? But he tried to push these thoughts from his mind—after all, the sword was about destiny, not strength. And he forced himself to remember that it was his destiny to be here, to be the firstborn of the MacGils, to be King. He searched the crowd for Argon; for some reason he had a sudden, intense desire to seek his counsel. This was the time he needed him most. For some reason, he could think of no one else. But of course, he was nowhere to be found.

Finally, the dozen men reached the center of the room, carrying the sword into the shaft of sunlight, and they placed it down on the iron prongs. It landed with a reverberating clang, the sound traveling in ripples throughout the room. The room fell entirely silent.

The crowd instinctively parted ways, making a path for Gareth to walk down and try to hoist it.

Gareth slowly rose from his throne, savoring the moment, savoring all this attention. He could feel all the eyes on him. He knew a moment like this would never come again, when the entire kingdom watched him so completely, so intensely, analyzing every move he made. He had lived this moment so many times in his mind since he had been a youth, and now it had come. He wanted it to go slowly.

He walked down the steps of the throne, taking them one at a time, savoring each step. He walked on the red carpet, feeling how soft it was beneath his feet, closer and closer towards the patch of sunlight, towards the sword. As he walked, it was like walking in a dream. He felt outside of himself. A part of him felt as if he had walked this carpet many times before, having hoisted the sword a million times in his dreams. It made him feel all the more that he was fated to hoist it, that he was walking into destiny.

He saw how it would go in his mind: he would step forward boldly, reach out with a single hand, and as his subjects leaned in, he would suddenly and dramatically raise it high over his head with a single hand. They would all gasp and fall to their faces and declare him the Chosen One, the most important of the MacGil kings who had ever ruled, the one meant to rule forever. They would weep with joy at the sight. They would cower in fear of him. They would thank the gods that they had lived in this lifetime to witness it. They would worship him as a god.

Gareth approached the sword, just feet away now, and felt himself tremble inside. As he entered the sunlight, although he had seen the sword many times before, he was taken aback by its beauty. He had never been allowed this close to it before, and it surprised him. It was intense. With a long shining blade, made from a material which no one had deciphered, it had the most ornate hilt he had ever seen, wrapped with a fine, silk-like material, encrusted with jewels of every sort, and emblazoned with the falcon crest. As he took a step closer, hovering over it, he felt the intense energy radiating off of it. It seemed to throb. He could hardly breathe. In just a moment it would be in his palm. High above his head. Shining in the sunlight for all the world to see.

He, Gareth, the Great One.

Gareth reached out and placed his right hand on the hilt, slowly closing it, feeling every jewel, every contour as he grasped it, electrified. An intense energy radiated through his palm, up his arm, through his body. It was unlike anything he had ever felt. He knew that this was his moment. His moment for all time.

Gareth reached down and clasped his other hand on the hilt, too. He closed his eyes, his breathing shallow.

If it please the gods, allow me to hoist this. Give me a sign. Show me that I am King. Show me that I am meant to rule.

Gareth prayed silently, waiting for a response, for a sign, for the perfect moment. But seconds went by, a full ten seconds, the entire kingdom watching, and he heard no response.

Then, suddenly, he saw the face of his father, scowling back at him.

Gareth opened his eyes in terror, wanting to wipe the image from his mind. His heart pounded, and he felt it was a terrible omen.

It was now or never.

Gareth leaned over, and with all his might, he tried to hoist the sword. He struggled for all he had, until his entire body shook, convulsed.

The sword did not budge. It was like trying to move the very foundation of the earth.

Gareth tried harder still, harder, and harder. Finally, he was visibly groaning and screaming.

Moments later, he collapsed.

The blade had not moved an inch.

A shocked gasp spread throughout the room as he hit the ground. Several advisers rushed to his aid, checking to see if he was okay, and he violently shoved them away. Embarrassed, he stood, bringing himself back to his own two feet.

Humiliated, Gareth looked around at his subjects, looking to see how they would view him now.

They had already turned away, were already filtering from the room. Gareth could see the disappointment in their faces, could see that he was just another failed spectacle in their eyes. Now they all knew, each and every one of them, that he was not their true king. He was not the destined and chosen MacGil. He was nothing. Just another prince who had usurped the throne.

Gareth felt himself burning with shame. He had never felt more lonely than in that moment. Everything he had imagined, from the time he was a child, had been a lie. A delusion. He had believed in his own fable.

And it had crushed him.

CHAPTER SIX

Gareth paced in his chamber, his mind reeling, stunned by his failure to hoist the sword, trying to process the ramifications. He felt numb. He could hardly believe he had been so stupid to attempt to hoist the sword, the Dynasty Sword, which no MacGil had been able to hoist for seven generations. Why had he thought he would be better than his ancestors? Why had he assumed he would be different?

He should have known. He should have been cautious, never should have overestimated himself. He should have been content with simply having his father's throne. Why he had he had to push it?

Now all his subjects knew he was not the Chosen One; now his rule would be marred by this; now, perhaps, they would have more grounds to suspect him for the death of his father. He saw that everyone looked at him differently already, as if he were a walking ghost, as if they were already preparing themselves for the next king to come.

Worse than that, for the first time in his life, Gareth felt unsure about himself. His entire life, he had seen his destiny clearly. He had been certain he was meant to take his father's place, to rule and to wield the sword. His confidence had been shaken to the core. Now, he was not sure about anything.

Worst of all, he could not stop seeing that image of his father's face, right before he'd hoisted it. Had that been his revenge?

"Bravo," came a slow, sardonic voice.

Gareth spun, shocked that anyone was with him in this chamber. He recognized the voice instantly; it was a voice he had become too familiar with over the years, and one he had come to despise. It was the voice of his wife.

Helena.

There she stood, in a far corner of the room, observing him as she reached up and smoked her opium pipe. She inhaled deeply, held it, then slowly let it out. Her eyes were bloodshot, and he could see that she had been smoking too long.

"What are you doing here?" he asked.

"This is my bridal chamber after all," she responded. "I can do anything I want here. I'm your wife and your queen. Don't forget. I rule this kingdom as much as you do. And after your debacle today, I would use the term *rule* very loosely indeed."

Gareth's face burned red. Helena had always had a way of striking him with the lowest blow of all, and at the most inopportune time. He despised her more than any woman in his life. He could hardly conceive that he had agreed to marry her.

"Do you?" Gareth spat, turning and marching towards her, seething. "You forget that I am King, you wench, and I could have you imprisoned, just like anyone else in my kingdom, whether you are my wife or not."

She laughed at him, a derisive snort.

"And then what?" she snapped. "Have your new subjects wonder of your sexuality? No, I doubt that very much. Not in the scheming world of Gareth. Not in the mind of the man who cares more than anyone else how people perceive him."

Gareth stopped before her, realizing she had a way of seeing through him which annoyed him to the core. He understood her threat, and he realized that arguing with her would do no good. So he just stood there, quietly, waiting, his fists bunched.

"What is it that you want?" he said slowly, trying to control himself from doing something rash. "You don't come to me unless you want something."

She laughed, a dry, mocking laugh.

"I'll take whatever it is that I want. I haven't come to ask you for anything. But rather to tell you something: your entire kingdom has just witnessed your failure to hoist the sword. Where does that leave us?"

"What you mean *us*?" he asked, wondering where she was going with this.

"Your people know now what I have always known: that you are failure. That you are not the Chosen One. Congratulations. At least now it is official."

He scowled back.

"My father failed to wield the sword. That did not prevent him from ruling effectively as King."

"But it affected his kingship," she snapped. "Every moment of it."

"If you're so unhappy with my inabilities," Gareth fumed, "why don't you just leave this place?

Leave me! Leave our mockery of a marriage. I am King now. I don't need you anymore."

"I'm glad you raised that point," she said, "because that is precisely the reason I've come. I want you to end our marriage officially. I want a divorce. There is a man I love. A *real* man. One of your knights, in fact. He's a warrior. We are in love, a true love. Unlike any love I ever had. Divorce me, so I can stop carrying on this affair in secret. I want our love to be public. And I want to be married to him."

Gareth stared back at her, shocked, feeling hollowed out, as if a dagger had just been plunged into his chest. Why had Helena had to surface? Why now, of all times? It was too much for him. He felt as if the world were kicking him while he was down.

Despite himself, Gareth was surprised to realize that he had some deep feelings for Helena, because when he heard her actual words, asking for a divorce, it did something to him. It upset him. Despite himself, it made him realize that he did not want a divorce from her. If it came from him, it was one thing; but if it came from her, it was another. He did not want her to have her way, and not so easily.

Most of all, he wondered how a divorce would influence his kingship. A divorced King would raise too many questions. And despite himself, he found himself jealous of this knight. And resentful of her rubbing his lack of manhood in his face. He wanted vengeance. On both of them.

"You can't have it," he snapped. "You are bound to me. Stuck as my wife forever. I will never

31

let you free. And if I ever encounter this knight you are cheating with, I will have him tortured and executed."

Helena snarled back at him.

"I am *not* your wife! You are not my husband. You are not a man. Ours is an unholy union. It has been from the day it was forged. It was an arranged partnership for power. The whole thing disgusts me—it always has. And it has ruined my one chance to *truly* be married."

She breathed, her fury rising.

"You will give me my divorce, or I will reveal to the entire kingdom the man you are. You decide."

With that Helena turned her back on him, marched across the room and out the open door, not even bothering to close it behind her.

Gareth stood alone in the stone chamber, listening to the echo of her footsteps and feeling a chill pervade his body that he could not shake. Was there anything stable he could hold onto anymore?

As Gareth stood there, trembling, watching the open door, he was surprised to see somebody else walk through it. He had barely had time to register his conversation with Helena, to process all of her threats, when in walked a too-familiar face. Firth. The usual bounce to his step was gone as he entered the room tentatively, a guilty look on his face.

"Gareth?" he asked, sounding unsure.

Firth stared at him, wide-eyed, and Gareth could see how bad he felt. He *should* feel bad, Gareth thought. After all, it was Firth who put him up to wielding the sword, who had finally convinced him, who had made him think that he was more than he was. Without Firth's whispering, who knew? Maybe Gareth would have never even attempted to wield it.

Gareth turned to him, seething. In Firth he finally found an object in which to direct all his anger. After all, Firth had been the one that killed his father. It was Firth, this stupid stable boy, that got him into this whole mess to begin with. Now he was just another failed successor to the MacGil lineage.

"I hate you," Gareth seethed. "What of your promises now? What of your confidence that I would wield the sword?"

Firth swallowed, looking very nervous. He was speechless. Clearly, he had nothing to say.

"I am sorry, my Lord," he said. "I was wrong."

"You were wrong about a lot of things," Gareth snapped.

Indeed, the more Gareth thought about it, the more he realized how wrong Firth had been. In fact, if it were not for Firth, his father would still be alive today—and Gareth would not be in any of this mess. The weight of the kingship would not be on his head, all these things would not be going wrong. Gareth longed for simpler days, when he was not King, when his father was alive. He felt a sudden desire to bring them all back, the way things used to be. But he could not. And he had Firth to blame for all of this.

"What is it you are doing here?" Gareth pressed.

Firth cleared his throat, obviously nervous.

"I've heard…rumors…whispers of servants talking. Word has reached me that your brother and sister are asking too many questions. They've been spotted in the servants' quarters. Examining the waste chute for the murder weapon. The dagger I used to kill your father."

Gareth's body went cold at his words. He was frozen in shock and fear. Could this day get any worse?

He cleared his throat.

"And what did they find?" he asked, his throat dry, the words barely escaping.

Firth shook his head.

"I do not know, my lord. All I know is that they suspect something."

Gareth felt a renewed hatred for Firth, one he did not know he was capable of. If it wasn't for his bumbling ways, if he had disposed of the weapon properly, he would not be in this position. Firth had left him vulnerable.

"I'm only going to say this once," Gareth said, stepping close to Firth, getting in his face, glowering back at him with the firmest look he could muster. "I do not want to see your face ever again. Do you understand me? Leave my presence, and never come back. I'm going to relegate you to a position far from here. And if you ever step foot in these castle walls again, rest assured I will have you arrested.

"NOW LEAVE!" Gareth shrieked.

Firth, eyes welling with tears, turned and fled the room, his footsteps echoing long after he ran down the corridor.

Gareth drifted back to thinking of the sword, of his failed attempt. He could not help but feel as if he had set in motion a great calamity for himself. He felt as if he had just pushed himself off a cliff, and from here on in, he would only be facing his descent.

He stood there, rooted to the stone in the reverberating silence, in his father's chamber, trembling, wondering what on earth he had set in motion. He had never felt so alone, so unsure of himself.

Was this what it meant to be king?

*

Gareth hurried up the stone, spiral staircase, rushing up floor after floor, hurrying his way to the castle's uppermost parapets. He needed fresh air. He needed time and space to think. He needed a vantage point of his kingdom, a chance to see his court, his people, and to remember that it was all *his*. That, despite all the nightmarish events of the day, he, after all, was still king.

Gareth had dismissed his attendants and he ran alone, up flight after flight, breathing hard. He stopped on one of the floors, bent over and caught his breath. Tears were streaming down his cheeks. He kept seeing the face of his father, scolding him at every turn.

"I hate you!" he screamed to the empty air.

He could have sworn he heard mocking laughter in return. His father's laughter.

Gareth needed to get away from here. He turned and continued running, sprinting, until finally he reached the top. He burst out through the door, and the fresh summer air hit him in the face.

He breathed deep, catching his breath, reveling in the sunshine, in the warm breezes. He took off his mantle, his father's mantle, and threw it down to the ground. It was too hot—and he didn't want to wear it anymore.

He hurried to the edge of the parapet and clutched the stone wall, breathing hard, looking down on his court. He could see the never-ending crowd, filtering out from the castle. They were leaving the ceremony. His ceremony. He could almost feel their disappointment from here. They looked so small. He marveled that they were all under his control.

But for how long?

"Kingships are funny things," came an ancient voice.

Gareth spun and saw, to his surprise, Argon standing there, feet away, wearing a white cloak and hood and holding his staff. He stared back at him, a smile at the corner of his lips—yet his eyes were not smiling. They were glowing, staring right through him, and they set Gareth on edge. They saw too much.

There were so many things Gareth had wanted to say to Argon, to ask him. But now that he had already failed to wield the sword, he could not recall a single one.

"Why didn't you tell me?" Gareth pleaded, desperation in his voice. "You could have told me I was not meant to hoist it. You could have saved me the shame."

"And why would I do that?" Argon asked.

Gareth scowled.

36

"You are not a true counsel to the King," he said. "You would have counseled my father truly. But not I."

"Perhaps he was deserving of true counsel," Argon replied.

Gareth's fury deepened. He hated this man. And he blamed him.

"I don't want you around me," Gareth said. "I don't know why my father hired you, but I don't want you in King's Court."

Argon laughed, a hollow, scary sound.

"Your father did not hire me, foolish boy," he said. "Nor his father before him. I was meant to be here. In fact, you might say I hired them."

Argon suddenly took a step forward, and looked as if he were staring into Gareth's soul.

"Can the same be said of you?" Argon asked. "Are you meant to be here?"

His words struck a nerve in Gareth, sent a chill through him. It was the very thing Gareth had been wondering himself. Gareth wondered if it was a threat.

"He who reigns by blood will rule by blood," Argon proclaimed, and with those words, he swiftly turned his back and began to walk away.

"Wait!" Gareth screamed, no longer wanting him to go, needing answers. "What do you mean by that?"

Gareth could not help but feel that Argon was giving him a message, that he would not rule long. He needed to know if that was what he had meant.

Gareth ran after him, but as he approached, he could hardly believe what happened: right before his eyes, Argon disappeared.

Gareth turned, looked all around him, but saw nothing. He heard only a hollow laughter, somewhere in the air.

"Argon!" Gareth screamed.

He turned again, then looked up to the heavens, sinking to one knee and throwing back his head. He shrieked:

"ARGON!"

CHAPTER SEVEN

Erec marched alongside the Duke, Brandt and dozens of the Duke's entourage, through the winding streets of Savaria, a crowd growing as they went, towards the house of the servant girl. Erec had insisted that he meet her without delay, and the Duke had wanted to lead the way personally. And when the Duke came, everyone followed. Erec looked around at the huge and growing entourage, and was embarrassed, realizing he would arrive at this girl's abode with dozens of people in tow.

Since he had first seen her, Erec had been able to think of little else. Who was this girl, he wondered, who seemed so noble, yet worked as a servant in the Duke's court? Why had she fled from him so hastily? Why was it that, in all his years, with all the royal women he had met, this was the only one who had captured his heart?

Being around royalty his entire life, the son of a king himself, Erec could detect other royalty in an instant—and he sensed from the moment he spotted her that she was of a much more regal position than the one she was occupying. He was burning with curiosity to know who she was, where she was from, what she was doing here. He needed another chance to set his eyes upon her, to see if he had been imagining it or if he would still feel the way he did.

"My servants tell me she lives on the city's outskirts," the Duke explained, talking as they walked. As they went, people on all sides of the streets opened their shutters and looked down, amazed at the presence of the Duke and his entourage in the common streets.

"Apparently, she is servant to an innkeeper. Nobody knows her origin, where she came from. All they know is that she arrived in our city one day, and became an indentured servant to this innkeeper. Her past, it seems, is a mystery."

They all turned down another side street, the cobblestone beneath them becoming more crooked, the small dwellings closer to each other and more dilapidated, as they went. The Duke cleared his throat.

"I took her in as a servant in my court on special occasions. She is quiet, keeps to herself. No one knows much about her. Erec," the Duke said, finally turning to Erec, laying a hand on his wrist, "are you certain about this? This woman, whoever she is, is just another commoner. You can have your choice of any woman in the kingdom."

Erec looked back at him with equal intensity.

"I must see this girl again. I don't care who she is."

The Duke shook his head in disapproval, and they all continued walking, turning down street after street, passing through twisting, narrow alleyways. As they went, this neighborhood of Savaria became even seedier, the streets filled with drunken types, lined with filth, chickens and wild dogs roaming about. They passed tavern after tavern, the screams

40

of patrons carrying out into the streets. Several drunks stumbled before them, and as night began to fall, the streets began to be lit by torches.

"Make way for the Duke!" screamed his lead attendant, rushing forward and finally pushing drunks out of the way. All up and down the streets unsavory types parted ways and watched, amazed, as the Duke passed, Erec beside him.

Finally, they arrived at a small, humble inn, built of stucco, with a pitched, slate roof. It looked as if it could hold maybe fifty patrons in its tavern below, with a few rooms for guests above. The front door was crooked, one window was broken, and its entry lamp hung crookedly, its torch flickering, the wax too low. Screams of drunks spilled out the windows, as they all they stopped before the door.

How could such a fine girl work in a place like this? Erec wondered, horrified, as he heard the shouts and jeers from inside. His heart broke as he thought of it, as he thought of the indignity she must suffer in such a place. *It's not fair,* he thought. He felt determined to rescue her from it.

"Why do you come to the worst possible place to choose a bride?" the Duke asked, turning to Erec.

Brandt turned to him too.

"Last chance, my friend," Brandt said. "There is a castle full of royal women waiting for you back there."

But Erec shook his head, determined.

"Open the door," he commanded.

One of the Duke's men rushed forward and yanked it open. The smell of stale ale came out in waves, making him recoil.

Inside, drunken men were hunched over the bar, seated along wooden tables, screaming too loudly, laughing, jeering and jostling each other. They were crude types, Erec could see that at once, with bellies too large, cheeks unshaven, clothes unwashed. None of them warriors.

Erec took several steps in, searching the place for her. He could not possibly imagine that a woman like her could work in such a place. He wondered if maybe they had come to the wrong dwelling.

"Excuse me, sir, I'm looking for a woman," Erec said to the man standing beside him, tall and wide, with a big belly, unshaven.

"Are you then?" the man yelled out, mocking. "Well, you've come to the wrong place! This is not a brothel. Although there is one across the street—and I hear the women there are fine and plump!"

The man started laughing, too loudly, in Erec's face, and several of his fellows joined in.

"It is not a brothel I seek," Erec answered, unamused, "but a single woman, one who works here."

"You must mean then the innkeeper's servant," called out someone else, another large, drunk man. "She's probably in the back somewhere, scrubbing the floors. Too bad—I wish she were up here, on my lap!"

The men all screamed out in laughter, overwhelmed with their own jokes, and Erec reddened at the thought of it. He felt ashamed for her. For her to have to serve all of these types—it was an indignity that was too much for him to contemplate.

"And you are?" came another voice.

A man stepped forward, wider than the others, with a dark beard and eyes, a deep scowl, a wide jaw, accompanied by several seedy men. He had more muscle on him than fat, and he approached Erec threateningly, clearly territorial.

"Are you trying to steal my servant girl?" he demanded. "Out with you then!"

He stepped forward and reached out to grab Erec.

But Erec, hardened by years of training, the kingdom's greatest knight, had reflexes beyond what this man could imagine. The moment his hands touched Erec, he sprang into action, grabbing his wrist in a lock, spinning the man around with lightning speed, grabbing him by the back of his shirt, and shoving him across the room.

The big man went flying like a cannonball, and he took several men out with him, all of them crashing to the floor of the small place like bowling pins.

The entire room grew silent, as every man stopped and watched.

"FIGHT! FIGHT!" the men chanted.

The innkeeper, dazed, stumbled to his feet and charged for Erec with a shout.

This time Erec did not wait. He stepped forward to meet his attacker, raised an arm, and brought his elbow straight down on the man's face, breaking his nose as he charged.

The innkeeper stumbled backwards, then collapsed, landing on the floor on his rear.

Erec stepped forward, picked him up, and despite his size, hoisted him high above his head. He took several steps forward and threw the man, and he went flying through the air, taking half the room down with him.

All the men in the room froze, stopping their chanting, growing quiet, starting to realize that someone special was among them. The bartender, though, suddenly came rushing forward, a glass bottle held high over his head, aiming right for Erec.

Erec saw it coming and already had his hand on his sword—but before Erec could draw it, his friend Brandt stepped forward, beside him, drew a dagger from his belt, and held the tip of it out at the bartender's throat.

The bartender ran right into it and stopped cold, the blade just about to puncture his skin. He stood there, eyes wide open in fear, sweating, frozen in mid-air with the bottle. The room grew so silent at the standoff one could hear a pin drop.

"Drop it," Atme ordered.

The bartender did so, and the bottle smashed on the floor.

Erec drew his sword with a resounding ring of metal and walked over to the innkeeper, who lay moaning on the floor, and pointed it at his throat.

"I will only say this once," Erec announced. "Clear this room of all this riffraff. Now. I demand an audience with the lady. Alone."

"The Duke!" someone yelled.

The whole room turned and finally recognized the Duke standing there, by the entrance, flanked by his men. All of them rushed to take off their caps and bow their heads.

"If the room is not clear by the time I finish speaking," the Duke announced, "each one of you here will be imprisoned at once."

The room broke into a frenzy as all the men inside scurried to vacate, rushing past the Duke and out the front door, leaving their unfinished bottles of ale where they were.

"And out with you, too," Brandt said to the bartender, lowering his dagger, grabbing him by his hair and shoving him out the door.

The room, which had been so rowdy moments before, now sat empty, silent, save for Erec, Brandt, the Duke, and a dozen of his closest men. They shut the door behind them with a resounding slam.

Erec turned to the innkeeper, sitting on the floor, still dazed, wiping blood from his nose. Erec grabbed him by the shirt, hoisted him up with both hands, and sat him down on one of the empty benches.

"You've ruined my business for the night," the innkeeper whined. "You will pay for this."

The Duke stepped forward and backhanded him.

"I can have you killed for attempting to lay a hand on this man," the Duke scolded. "Do you not know who this is? This is Erec, the king's best knight, the champion of The Silver. If he chooses to, he can kill you himself, right now."

The innkeeper looked up at Erec, and for the first time, real fear crossed his face. He nearly trembled in his seat.

"I had no idea. You did not announce yourself."

"Where is she?" Erec demanded, impatient.

"She's in the back, scrubbing the kitchen. What is it that you want with her? Did she steal something of yours? She is just another indentured servant girl."

Erec drew his dagger and held it to the man's throat.

"Call her a 'servant' again," Erec warned, "and you can be sure I will cut your throat. Do you understand?" he asked firmly as he held the blade against the man's skin.

The man's eyes flooded with tears, as slowly he nodded.

"Bring her here, and hurry about it," Erec ordered, and yanked him to his feet and gave him a shove, sending him flying across the room, and towards the back door.

As the innkeeper left, there came a clanging of pots from behind the door, muted yelling, and then, moments later, the door opened, and out came several women, dressed in rags, smocks and bonnets, covered in kitchen grease. There were three older women, in their sixties, and Erec wondered for a moment if the innkeeper knew who he was speaking of.

And then, she came out—and Erec's heart stopped in his chest.

He could hardly breathe. It was her.

She wore an apron, covered in grease stains, and she kept her head down low, ashamed to look up. Her hair was tied, covered in a cloth, her cheeks were caked with dirt—and yet still, Erec was smitten by her. Her skin was so young, so perfect. She had high, chiseled cheeks and jawbones, a small nose covered in freckles, and full lips. She had a broad, regal forehead, and her beautiful blonde hair spilled out from beneath the bonnet.

She glanced up at him, just for a moment, and her large, wonderful almond-green eyes, which shifted in the light, changing to crystal blue then back again, held him rooted in place He was surprised to realize that he was even more mesmerized by her now than he had been when he'd first met her.

Behind her, out came the innkeeper, scowling, still wiping blood from his nose. The girl walked forward tentatively, surrounded by these older women, towards Erec, and curtsied as she got close. Erec rose, standing before her, as did several of the Duke's entourage.

"My lord," she said, her voice soft, sweet, filling Erec's heart. "Please tell me what I've done to offend you. I don't know what it is, but I'm sorry for whatever it is I have done to warrant the presence of the Duke's court."

Erec smiled. Her words, her language, the sound of her voice—it all made him feel restored. He never wanted her to stop speaking.

Erec reached up and touched her chin with his hand, lifting it until her gentle eyes looked at his. His heart raced as he looked into her eyes. It was like getting lost in a sea of blue.

"My lady, you have done nothing to offend. I do not think you shall ever be able to offend. I come here not out of anger—but out of love. Since I saw you, I have been able to think of nothing else."

The girl looked flustered, and immediately dropped her eyes to the ground, blinking several times. She twisted her hands, looking nervous, overwhelmed. She was clearly unused to this.

"Please my lady, tell me. What is your name?"

"Alistair," she answered, humbly.

"Alistair," Erec repeated, overwhelmed. It was the most beautiful name he had ever heard.

"But I do not know why it should serve you to know it," she added, softly, still looking at the floor. "You are a Lord. And I am but a servant."

"She is *my* servant, to be exact," the innkeeper said, stepping forward, nasty. "She is indentured to me. She signed a contract, years ago. Seven years is what she promised. In return, I give her food and board. She is three years in. So you see, this is all a waste of time. She is mine. I own her. You are not taking this one away. She is mine. Do you understand?"

Erec felt a hatred for the innkeeper beyond what he had ever felt for a man. He was partly of a mind to draw his sword and stab him in the heart and be done with him. But however much the man may have deserved it, Erec did not want to break the King's law. After all, his actions reflected on the king.

48

"The King's law is the King's law," Erec said to the man, firmly. "I don't intend on breaking it. That said, tomorrow begin the tournaments. And I am entitled, as any man, to choose my bride. And let it be known here and now that I choose Alistair."

A gasp spread the room, as everyone turned to each other, shocked.

"That is," Erec added, "if she consents."

Erec looked at Alistair, his heart pounding, as she kept her face lowered to the floor. He could see that she was blushing.

"Do you consent, my lady?" he asked.

The room fell silent.

"My Lord," she said softly, "you know nothing of who I am, of where I am from, of why I am here. And I am afraid these are things I cannot tell you."

Erec stared back, puzzled.

"Why can you not tell me?"

"I have never told anyone since my arrival. I have made a vow."

"But why?" he pressed, so curious.

But Alistair merely kept her face down, silent.

"It's true," inserted one of the servant women. "This one's never told us who she is. Or why she's here. She refuses to. We've tried for years."

Erec was deeply puzzled by her—but that only added to her mystery.

"If I cannot know who you are, then I shall not," Erec said. "I respect your vow. But that will not change my affection for you. My lady, whoever you are, if I should win these tournaments, then I will choose you as my prize. You, from any woman in this entire kingdom. I ask you again: do you consent?"

Alistair kept her eyes fixed to the ground, and as Erec watched, he saw tears rolling down her cheeks.

Suddenly, she turned and fled from the room, running out and closing the door behind her.

Erec stood there, with the others, in the stunned silence. He hardly knew how to interpret her response.

"You see then, you waste your time, and mine," the innkeeper said. "She said no. Be off with you then."

Erec frowned back.

"She did not say no," Brandt interjected. "She did not respond."

"She is entitled to take her time," Erec said, in her defense. "After all, it is a lot at once. She does not know me, either."

Erec stood there, debating what to do.

"I will stay here tonight," Erec finally announced. "You shall give me a room here, down the hall from hers. In the morning, before the tournaments begin, I shall ask her again. If she consents, and if I win, she shall be my bride. If so, I will buy her out of her servitude with you, and she shall leave this place with me."

The innkeeper clearly did not want Erec under his roof, but he dared not say anything; so he turned and stormed from the room, slamming the door behind him.

"Are you certain you wish to stay here?" the Duke asked. "Come back to the castle with us."

Erec nodded back, gravely.

"I have never been more certain of anything in my life."

CHAPTER EIGHT

Thor plummeted down through the air, diving, racing head first for the churning waters of the Sea of Fire. He entered it and sunk down, immersed, and was startled to feel the water was hot.

Beneath the surface, Thor opened his eyes briefly—and wished he hadn't. He caught a glimpse of all manner of strange and ugly sea creatures, small and big, with unusual and grotesque faces. This ocean was teeming. He prayed they did not attack him before he could reach the safety of the rowboat.

Thor surfaced with a gasp, and looked immediately for the drowning boy. He spotted him, and just in time: he was flailing, sinking, and in a few more seconds, surely he would have drowned.

Thor reached around, grabbed him from behind by his collarbone, and began to swim with him, keeping both of their heads above water. Thor heard a whelp and a whine, and as he turned, he was shocked to see Krohn: he must have leapt in after him. He swam beside him, paddling up to Thor, whining. Thor felt terrible that Krohn was endangered like this—but his hands were full and there was little he could do.

Thor tried not to look all around him, at the waters, churning red, at the strange creatures surfacing and disappearing all around him. An ugly looking creature, purple, with four arms and two heads, surfaced nearby, hissed at him, then submerged, making Thor flinch.

Thor turned and saw the rowboat, about twenty yards away, and he swam for it frantically, using his one arm and his legs as he dragged the boy. The boy flailed and screamed, resisting, and Thor feared he might bring him down with him.

"Hold still!" Thor screamed harshly, hoping the boy would listen.

Finally, he did. Thor was momentarily relieved—until he heard a splash and turned his head the other way: right beside him, another creature surfaced, small, with a yellow head and four tentacles. It had a square head, and it swam right up to him, snarling and shaking. It looked like a rattlesnake that lived in the sea, except its head was too square. Thor braced himself as it got closer, preparing to be bit—but then suddenly it opened its mouth wide and spat seawater at him. Thor blinked, trying to get it from his eyes.

The creature swam around and around them, in circles, and Thor redoubled his efforts, swimming faster, trying to get away from it.

Thor was making progress, getting closer to the boat, when suddenly another creature surfaced, on his other side. It was long, narrow and orange, with two claws at its mouth and dozens of small legs. It also had a long tail, which it whipped about in every direction. It looked like a lobster, standing upright. It skirted along the water's edge, like a water bug, and buzzed its way close to Thor, turning to the side and whipping its tail. The tail lashed Thor's arm, and he cried out in pain—it stung.

The creature whizzed back and forth, lashing out again and again. Thor wished he could draw his sword and attack it—but he only had one free hand, and he needed it to swim.

Krohn, swimming beside him, turned and snarled at the creature, a hair-raising noise, and as Krohn fearlessly swam its way, it scared the beast, making it disappear beneath the waters. Thor sighed with relief—until the creature suddenly reappeared on his other side, and lashed him again. Krohn turned and chased it all around, trying to catch it, snapping his jaws at it, and always missing.

Thor swam for his life, realizing the only way out of this mess was to get out of this sea. After what felt like forever, swimming harder than he'd ever had, he swam up close to the rowboat, rocking violently in the waves. As he did, two Legion members, older boys who never spoke to Thor and his classmates, were waiting there to help him. To their credit, they leaned over and extended him a hand.

Thor helped the boy first, reaching around and hoisting up towards the boat. The older boys grabbed the boy by his arms and dragged him up.

Thor then reached around, grabbed Krohn by his stomach and threw him up out of the water, and onto the boat. Krohn clamored with all four paws as he scratched and slipped on the wooden boat, dripping wet, shaking. He slid across the wet bottom, across the boat. Then he immediately pounced back up, turned, and ran back to the ledge, looking for Thor. He stood there, looking down into the water, and yelped.

Thor reached up and grabbed the hand of one of the boys, and was just pulling himself into the boat when suddenly he felt something strong and muscular wrap itself around his ankle and thigh. He turned and looked down, and his heart froze as he saw a lime-green squid-like creature, wrapping a tentacle around his leg.

Thor cried out in pain as he felt its stingers pierce his flesh.

Thor realized that if he didn't do something quick, he would be finished. With his free hand, he reached down to his belt, extracted a short dagger, leaned over, and slashed at it. But the tentacle was so thick, the dagger could not even pierce it.

It made it angry. The creature's head suddenly surfaced—green, with no eyes and two jaws on its long neck, one atop the other—opened its rows of razor-sharp teeth and leaned in towards Thor. Thor felt the blood being cut off from his leg, and knew he had to act fast. Despite the elder boy's efforts to hang onto him, Thor's grip was slipping, and he was sinking back into the water.

Krohn yelped and yelped, hairs standing on his back, leaning over as if getting ready to pounce into the water. But even Krohn must have known it would be useless to attack this thing.

One of the older boys stepped forward and screamed:

"DUCK!"

Thor lowered his head, as the boy threw a spear. It whizzed through the air but it missed, flew harmlessly by and sank into the water. The creature was too skinny, and too quick.

Suddenly, Krohn leapt off the boat and back into the water, landing with his jaws open and his sharp teeth extended on the back of the creature's neck. Krohn clamped down and swung the creature left and right, not letting go.

But it was a losing battle: the creature's skin was too tough, and it was too muscular. The creature threw Krohn side to side then finally sent him flying into the water. Meanwhile, the creature's grip tightened on Thor's leg; it was like a vice, and Thor felt himself losing oxygen. The tentacles burned so bad, Thor felt as if his leg was about to be torn off his body.

In one final, desperate attempt, Thor let go of the boy's hand and in the same motion swung around and reached for the short sword on his belt.

But he could not grab it in time; he slipped and spun and fell face first into the water.

Thor felt himself dragged away, farther from the boat, the creature pulling him out to sea. He was dragged backwards, faster and faster, and as he reached out helplessly, he watched the rowboat disappearing before him. The next thing he knew, he felt himself being pulled down, beneath the surface of the water, deep into the depths of the Sea of Fire.

CHAPTER NINE

Gwendolyn ran in the open meadow, her father, King MacGil, beside her. She was young, maybe ten, and her father was much younger, too. His beard was short, not showing any signs of the gray it would have later in life, and his skin was free of wrinkles, youthful, shining. He was happy, carefree, and laughed with abandon as he held her hand and ran with her through the fields. This was the father she remembered, the father she knew.

He picked her up and threw her over his shoulder, spinning her again and again, laughing louder and louder, and she giggled hysterically. She felt so safe in his arms, and she wanted this time together to never end.

But when her father set her down, something strange happened. Suddenly, the day went from a sunny afternoon to twilight. When Gwen's feet hit the ground, they were no longer in the flowers of the meadow, but stuck in mud, up to her ankles. Her father now lay in the mud, on his back, a few feet away from her, older, much older, too old, and he was stuck. A few feet away, lying in the mud, was his crown, sparkling.

"Gwendolyn," he gasped. "My daughter. Help me."

He lifted a hand out from the mud, reaching for her, desperate.

She was overcome with an urgency to help him, and she tried to go to him, to grab his hand. But her feet would not budge. She looked down and saw that they were stuck in the mud which was hardening all around her, drying up, cracking. She wiggled and wiggled, trying to break free.

Gwen blinked and found herself standing on the parapets of the castle, looking down on King's Court. Something was wrong: as she looked down, she did not see the usual splendor and festivities, but rather a sprawling cemetery. Where there once sat the shining splendor of King's Court there now sat fresh graves as far the eye could see.

She heard a shuffling of feet, and her heart stopped as she turned to see an assassin, wearing a black cloak and hood, approaching her. He sprinted for her, pulling back his hood, revealing a grotesque face, one eye missing, a thick, jagged scar over the socket. He snarled, raised one hand, and raised a glistening dagger, its hilt glowing red.

He was moving too fast and she could not react in time. She braced herself, knowing she was about to be killed as he brought the dagger down with full force.

It stopped suddenly, just inches from her face, and she opened her eyes to see her father, standing there, a corpse, catching the man's wrist in mid-air. He squeezed the man's hand until he dropped it, then hoisted the man over his shoulders and threw him off the parapet. Gwen listened to his screams as he plunged down over the edge.

Her father turned and stared at her, a corpse, his flesh decomposed; he grabbed her shoulders firmly, and wore a stern expression.

"It is not safe for you here," he warned. "It is not safe!" he screamed, his hands digging into her shoulders way too firmly, making her cry out.

Gwen woke screaming. She sat upright in bed, looking all around her chamber, expecting there to be an attacker.

But she was met with nothing but silence, the thick, still silence that preceded dawn.

Sweating, breathing hard, she jumped from bed, dressed in her nighttime lace, and paced her room. She hurried over to her small, stone basin and splashed water in her face, again and again. She leaned against the wall, felt the cool stone on her bare feet on this warm summer morning, and tried to compose herself.

The dream had felt too real. She sensed it was more than a dream—a genuine warning from her father, a message. She felt an urgency to leave King's Court, right now, and to never come back.

She knew that was something she could not do. She knew she had to compose herself, to gain her wits. But every time she blinked, she saw her father's face, felt his warning. She had to do something to shake the dream off.

Gwen looked out and saw the first sun just beginning to rise, and she thought of the only place that would help her regain her composure: King's River. Yes, she had to go.

*

Gwendolyn immersed herself again and again in the freezing cold springs of King's River, holding her nose and ducking her head under water. She sat in the small, natural swimming pool carved from rock, hidden in the upper springs, that she had found and frequented ever since she was a child. She held her head beneath the water and lingered there, feeling the cold currents run through her hair, over her scalp, feeling it wash and cleanse her naked body.

She had found this secluded spot one day, hidden amidst a clump of trees, high up on the mountain, a small plateau where the river slowed. In this spot, the river's current slowed, and the pool was deep and still. Above her, the river trickled in and below her, it continued to trickle down—yet here, on this plateau, the waters held just the slightest current. The pool was deep, the rocks smooth, and the place so well hidden, she could bathe naked with abandon. She came here almost every morning in the summer, as the sun was rising, to clear her mind. Especially on days like today, when dreams haunted her, as they often did, it was her one place of refuge.

It was so hard for Gwen to know if it was just a dream, or something more. How was she to know when a dream was a message, an omen? To know when it was just her mind playing tricks on her, or if she were being given a chance to take action?

Gwendolyn rose for air, breathing in the warm summer morning, hearing the birds chirp all around her in the trees. She leaned back against the rock, her body immersed up to her neck, sitting on a natural ledge in the water, thinking. She reached up with her hands and splashed her face, then ran her hands through her long, strawberry hair. She looked down at the crystal surface of the water, reflecting the sky, the second sun, which was already beginning to rise, the trees which arched over the water, and her own face. Her almond eyes, glowing blue, glowed back at her through the ripples. She could see something of her father in them. She turned away, thinking again of her dream.

She knew it was dangerous for her to remain in King's Court with her father's assassination, with all the spies, all the plots—and especially, with Gareth as king. Her brother was unpredictable. Vindictive. Paranoid. And very, very jealous. He saw everyone as a threat—especially her. Anything could happen. She knew that she was not safe here. Nobody was.

But she was not one to run. She needed to know for sure who her father's murderer was, and if it was Gareth, she could not run away until she had brought him to justice. She knew that her father's spirit would not rest until whoever killed him was caught. Justice had been his rallying cry all his life, and he, of all people, deserved to have it for himself in death.

Gwen thought again of her encounter with Godfrey and Steffen. She felt certain Steffen was hiding something, and wondered what it was. A part of her felt he might open up on his own time. But what if he would not? She felt an urgency to find her father's killer—but did not know where else to look.

Gwendolyn finally rose from her seat beneath the water, climbed onto shore naked, shivering in the morning air, hid behind a thick tree, and reached up to take her towel from a branch, as she always did.

But as she reached for it, she was shocked to discover her towel was not there. She stood there, naked, wet, and could not understand it. She was certain she had hung it there, as she always did.

As she stood there, baffled, shivering, trying to understand what had happened, suddenly, she sensed motion behind her. It happened so quick, a blur, and a moment later, her heart stopped, as she realized a man stood behind her.

It happened too fast. In seconds the man, wearing a black cloak and hood, as in her dream, was behind her. He grabbed her from behind, reached up with a bony hand and clasped it over her mouth, muting her screams as he held her tight from behind. He reached around with his other hand and grabbed her by the waist, pulling her close and hoisting her off the ground.

She kicked in the air, trying to scream, until he set her down, still clasping her tight. She tried to break free from his grasp, but he was too strong. He reached around and Gwen was to see he held a dagger with a glowing red hilt—the same from her dream. It had been a warning after all.

She felt the blade pressed up against her throat, and he held it so tight that if she moved in any direction, her throat would be cut. Tears poured down her cheeks as she struggled to breathe. She was so mad at herself. She had been so stupid. She should have been more vigilant.

"Do you recognize my face?" he asked.

He leaned forward and she felt his hot, bad breath on her cheek, and saw his profile. Her heart stopped—it was the same face from her dream, the man with the missing eye and scar.

"Yes," she answered, her voice shaking.

It was a face she knew too well. She did not know his name, but she knew that he was an enforcer. A low class type, one of several who hung around her brother, Gareth, since he was a child. He was Gareth's messenger. Gareth sent him to anyone he wished to scare—or torture or kill.

"You are my brother's dog," she hissed back at him, defiant.

He smiled, revealing missing teeth.

"I am his messenger," he said. "And my message comes with a special weapon to help you remember it. His message to you today is to stop asking questions. It is one you will come to know well, because when I'm finished with you, the scar I will leave on that pretty face of yours will make you remember it for your entire life."

He snorted, then raised the knife high and began to bring it down for her face.

"NO!" Gwen shrieked.

She braced herself for the life-changing slash.

But as the blade came down, something happened. Suddenly, a bird screeched, swooped down from out of the sky, dove right for the man. She glanced up and recognized it at the last second:

Ephistopheles.

It swooped down, its claws out, and scratched the man's face as he was bringing down the blade.

The blade had just begun to slice Gwen's cheek, stinging her with its pain, when it suddenly changed directions; the man shrieked, dropping the blade and raising his hands. Gwen saw a white light flash in the sky, the sun shining behind the branches, and as Ephistopheles flew away, she knew, she just knew, that her father had sent her.

She wasted no time. She spun around, leaned back and, as her trainers had taught her to do, kicked the man hard in the solo plexus, taking perfect aim with her barefoot. He keeled over, feeling the strength of her legs as she drove her kick right through him. She'd had it drilled into her, from the time she was young, that she did not need to be strong to fend off an attacker. She just needed to use her strongest muscles—her thighs. And to take aim precisely.

As the man stood there, keeled over, she stepped forward, grabbed the back of his hair and raised her knee—again, with pinpoint precision—and connected perfectly on the bridge of his nose.

She heard a satisfied crack and felt his hot blood gush out, pour onto her leg, staining it; as he slumped to the ground, she knew she had broken his nose.

She knew she should finish him off for good, take that dagger and plunge it into his heart.

But she stood there, naked, and her instinct was to clothe herself and get out of here. She didn't want his blood on her hands, however much he may have deserved it.

So instead she reached down, grabbed his blade, chucked it into the river, and wrapped her clothes around herself. She prepared to flee, but before she did, she turned back, wound up, and kicked him as hard as she could in the groin.

He screamed out in pain, and curled up in a ball, like a wounded animal.

Inwardly she was shaking, feeling how close she had come to being killed, or at least maimed. She felt the cut stinging her cheek, and realized she would probably carry some scar, however light. She felt traumatized. But she did not let him show it. Because at the same time, she also felt a new strength welling up in her, the strength of her father, of seven generations of MacGil kings. And for the first time she realized that she, too, was strong. As strong as her brothers. As strong as any of them.

Before she turned away, she leaned down close so he could hear her amidst his groans.

"Come near me again," she growled to the man, "and I will kill you myself."

CHAPTER TEN

Thor felt himself getting sucked down beneath the water and knew that within moments he would be plunged to the depths and drowned—if he wasn't eaten alive first. He prayed to god with all that he had.

Please, don't let me die now. Not here. Not in this place. Not by this creature's hand.

Thor tried to summon his powers, whatever they were. He tried with all that he had, willed that special energy to flow through him, to help him defeat this creature. He closed his eyes and willed for it to work.

But it did not call when he summoned it. Nothing happened. He was just a regular boy, powerless, just like everybody else. Where were his powers when he needed them most? Were they real? Or had all those other times just been a fluke?

As he was beginning to lose consciousness, a series of images flashed through his mind. He saw King MacGil, as if he were right there with him, watching over him; he saw Argon; and then he saw Gwendolyn. It was that last face that gave him reason to live.

Suddenly, Thor heard a splash behind him, then heard the creature shriek. He turned, just before he descended beneath the surface, to see Reese, in the water beside him. His sword was drawn, and he held the creature's severed head in his hand. The creature's head, detached from its body, continued to scream, as yellow blood gushed from its body.

Slowly, Thor felt its grip loosening on his leg, as Reese reached over and yanked it free of him. Thor's leg felt as if it were on fire, and he hoped and prayed that no permanent damage had been done.

Thor felt Reese's arm around his shoulder, and felt himself dragged back towards the boat. Thor blinked, in and out of consciousness, dimly seeing the huge rolling waves of the churning sea, feeling them rise and fall all around him.

They made it, and Thor felt himself being hoisted up and onto the boat, the other boys yanking him and Krohn on board. Reese landed in the boat beside him, and finally, all were safe.

Thor lay there, on the floor of the boat, breathing hard, the boat rising and falling in the sea, waves crashing all around them.

"You okay?" Reese asked, sitting over him.

Thor looked up and saw Krohn leaning over, then felt him licking his face. Thor reached up and stroked his wet fur. Thor grabbed Reese's hand, and pulled himself up to a sitting position, trying to get his bearings.

He shook it off and looked down at his leg, and saw that the creature had left marks, burning through his clothing, the pants on one leg now just a shred of fabric. He could see the round marks where it had leached onto him, and he rubbed them, feeling the slight indents. But now that the tentacle was off of him, the burning was getting better by the second. He tried bending his knee and was able to.

Luckily, it was not as bad as it could have been, and it seemed to be healing fast.

"I owe you one," Thor said, smiling up at Reese.

Reese smiled back.

"I think we're even."

Thor looked around and saw several of the older boys rowing, trying to gain control as the boat rocked violently in the waves.

"HELP!" came a shout.

Thor turned and looked back to the big boat and saw several boys jumping off the edge—or being pushed off by Kolk and the other commanders. Among them he spotted O'Connor, Elden and the twins. They all landed in the waters with a splash, and they bobbed there, flailing. Some were better swimmers than others. Creatures of all different colors and shapes and sizes surfaced in the waters around them.

"HELP!" a boy screamed again, as a wide, flat scaly creature turned sideways and lashed its fins at him.

Reese crossed the boat, grabbed a bow and arrow, and aimed it down at the water, firing on the creatures. He missed.

But he gave Thor an idea, and he jumped into action. Thor looked down and was thrilled to see his trusted sling still stuck to his waistband; he grabbed it, inserted a smooth stone in it from his pouch, took aim, and hurled.

The rock flew through the air and hit the creature right on its head, knocking it off the Legion member, and making it swim away.

Thor heard another shout, and he turned to see O'Connor, a different creature perched on his back. This creature looked like a frog, but was black, with white dots, and ten times the size. Its long tongue protruded from its mouth and slipped down towards O'Connor's neck. It made a strange snarling noise, and opened its jaws wide. O'Connor looked back over his shoulder in terror.

All around O'Connor, boys were shooting arrows at it, but missing. Thor placed a stone, leaned back, took aim, and hurled it.

It was a perfect hit. The creature made a weird squealing noise, and then turned and glared at Thor. It hissed and then, to Thor's shock, it turned and hopped right towards him.

Thor could not believe how far this creature could jump: it went flying through the air, its legs spread wide, and was coming right for his face.

Thor immediately reloaded his sling and fired again.

He struck the creature with a second to spare, right before it reached the boat. He hit in mid-air, and it plunged down, sinking into the waters.

Thor breathed deeply.

"LOOK OUT!" came a scream.

Thor spun just in time to see a huge wave coming out of nowhere and crashing down on the boat. Thor raised his hands and screamed—but it was too late. It engulfed them all.

For a moment, Thor was underwater. The wave submerged their boat, rocked it violently, then disappeared just as quickly.

They came up for air, the boat still intact, bobbing back to the surface. Thor gasped, coughing and spitting out the salty water as others around him did as well. Luckily, their boat was big, and that wave had been mostly foam. Thor looked around and spotted Krohn, clinging to the edge, and rushed over and grabbed him, just before he slipped over.

Their boat level again, Thor turned and saw that they were bearing down on the island. They were close to shore, hardly twenty feet away, which brought him a sense of relief.

But at the same time he realized that the shore was comprised of a virtual minefield of jagged boulders. There was no safe, smooth place to land. The huge waves were cresting and crashing down on the rocks. Suddenly another wave came, their boat was lifted high, and all the boys in the boat screamed at once as they came crashing down, straight for the rocks.

There was no time to react. A moment later, their entire boat shattered against the rock, the impact strong enough to shake Thor's jaw, as their boat splintered into pieces. The boys were all thrown from the boat.

Thor went flying head over heel and found himself back in the water, the churning red sea all around him, flailing, trying to orient himself. This time Krohn was near him, and Thor managed to reach out and grab him. Another wave came and picked them up, and brought them crashing down.

Thor dodged, and narrowly missed landing against a sharp rock. But another wave was coming, and he knew he had to do something quick.

He spotted a boulder flatter than the others, and he swam for it. He reached it just as a wave was receding and tried to climb up onto it; but it was covered in a slimy moss, and he kept losing his grip. Another wave came and pushed him up onto it, crunching his stomach against it but also lifting him up high enough to reach its plateau.

Finally on top of the rock, Thor turned and searched the waters for Reese. He saw him, flailing down below, and scurried down the boulder and reached down to grab him. But he was just out of reach.

"Your bow!" Thor screamed.

Reese understood—he reached onto his back and pulled off his bow and held out one end to Thor. Thor grabbed it and used it to yank him up, onto the rock. He made it safely, just before another wave crashed over him.

"Thanks," Reese said, smiling. "Now I owe you one."

Thor smiled back.

The two of them turned and Thor lifted Krohn and stuffed him into his shirt as they jumped to the top of the next boulder, then to the top of next one. They went on like this, boulder to boulder, getting ever closer to shore, until finally Thor slipped off of one and went hurling down into the sea. But he was close to shore now, and when the next wave came, it propelled him even farther, and he found himself able to stand, the water up to his waist. He waded his way towards shore, a tiny, narrow strip of black sand, and one final wave pounded him on his back and propelled him all the way.

Thor collapsed on the sand, Reese beside him, Krohn jumping out of his shirt and laying down, too. Thor was physically and mentally exhausted. But he had made it. He could not believe it. He had made it.

He sat up and turned and saw his fellow Legion members in the water, all wading to shore, waves crashing on their backs, washing up all around him. Some followed in his footsteps, hopping boulder to boulder; others were just thrown in the waves, bracing themselves and doing their best to avoid the rocks. He could see O'Connor, Elden, the twins, and other boys he recognized, and was relieved to see they were okay.

Thor turned the other way, and looked up at the steep cliffs behind him, rising straight up into the sky, leading to the island, somewhere up there.

"Now what?" he asked Reese, realizing they were stranded on this narrow, rocky strip of shore.

"We climb," Reese responded.

Thor examined the cliffs again; they soared a hundred feet, and looked wet, covered in the ocean spray. He didn't see how they could.

"But how?" Thor asked.

Reese shrugged.

"We don't have much choice. We can't stay down here. This beach is too narrow, and the tide is rising—we will be engulfed by the waves soon enough if we don't move."

The waves were already encroaching, the small strip of beach narrowing, and Thor knew he was right: they didn't have much time to waste. He had no idea how they would climb this cliff, but he knew they had to try. There was no other option.

Thor stuffed Krohn back into his shirt, turned for the cliff wall, crammed his hands into whatever nooks and crannies he could find, found some crags for his feet, and began climbing straight up. Beside him, Reese did the same.

It was incredibly hard, the cliff nearly smooth, with only small crags in which to place his fingers and toes. Sometimes he found himself having to pull himself up by just the tips of a few fingers, pushing off with just the tips of his toes. He had only gone a few feet, and his arms and legs already shook. He looked up, and saw at least a hundred feet before him; he looked down and saw a ten foot drop to the sand below. He was breathing hard, and did not know how he would make it. Krohn whined inside his shirt, wriggling.

Reese climbed at the same rate, and he rested beside him, also looked down, and shared the same bewildered look.

Thor took another step, and as he did, he slipped. He slid several feet. Reese reached out for him, but it was too late.

Thor went flying backwards, through the air, hurling, bracing himself for a rough impact on the sand. Krohn yelped, jumping out, flying through the air beside him.

Thor heard the crashing of a wave, and luckily, the wave hit the sand just before impact. Thor landed in the water, splashing down, and was grateful that it had softened the blow.

He sat up, and watched as Reese, too, lost his grip and came flying down and landed in the water, not too far from him. The two of them sat there, and wondered. All around them, other boys were arriving on the shore, and also looked up in wonder.

Thor didn't see how they could make it to the top, how they could ever make it to the island.

O'Connor, wading onto the sand, stood there and examined the cliff for a good minute before he reached back and removed the bow from his shoulder. From his waist he removed a long bunch of rope, and as Thor watched, he tied the rope to the end of an arrow.

Before Thor could ask him what he was doing, O'Connor fired.

The arrow carried the rope, higher and higher through the air, until it reached the very top of the cliff and looped itself around a small tree. It was a perfect shot, the arrow falling cleanly over one end and sliding back down the mountain. O'Connor tugged at it, making sure it was stable; the tree bent but did not give. Thor was impressed.

"I'm not a complete waste," O'Connor said, with a proud smile.

The other Legion members crowded around him and his rope, as O'Connor began to climb it.

He pulled himself up relatively quickly and easily, climbing higher and higher, until he reached the top. When he did, he tied the arrow around the tree, providing a secure rope for the others.

"One at a time!" O'Connor called down.

"You go," Reese said to Thor.

"After you," Thor said.

Reese climbed up, and Thor waited until he reached the top, then followed. It was easy compared to climbing the rock face, and soon Thor reached the top.

He was sweating, breathing hard, beyond exhausted, and he collapsed on the grass as he reached the island. It was real, soft grass, and after what he had been through, he felt as if he had landed on the most luxurious of beds.

Thor lifted his head enough to look out at the sunset all around him, casting a mystical light onto this strange place. It was craggy, desolate, forlorn, covered in an eerie and unwelcoming mist. The mist seemed to taint everything, seemed to threaten to swallow him whole. It was hardly a place he would call welcoming.

Thor swallowed. This desolate place, in the middle of nowhere, at the top of the world, would be home for the next hundred days.

CHAPTER ELEVEN

Gwendolyn ran through the back streets of King's court, twisting and turning, trying to remember her way to the alehouse. She had only been here once in her life, when trying to retrieve Godfrey for some occasion, and she had never frequented this part of King's Court since. It was too seedy for her, and she felt uncomfortable from all the stares as the streets became populated with unruly types. It saddened her that Godfrey had wasted so much of his life here, in this place that was beneath him. It had put a stain on the honor of the royal family, and she knew he was better than that.

Tears still poured down her cheeks and her heart still pounded as she ran through her mind, again and again, what had just happened at the river. She reached up and felt the small cut on her cheek, still stinging, still fresh, and wondered if it would scar. Gwen looked down at her hand and saw it was covered in blood. She had not taken time to bandage it—but that was the least of it now. She realized how lucky she was not to have been killed or maimed; she thought of Ephistopheles, and felt certain her father had saved her. Looking back, she should have heeded her dream more carefully. But how? Dreams were still a mystery to her. She never quite knew the right course of action to take, even when it seemed clear.

She knew of Gareth's dog's reputation for butchery, knew how many people he had maimed for life and marveled that she had escaped. She grew cold thinking that Gareth had sent him to her. Her mind spun with the implications. Obviously he would not have sent him unless he had something to hide about their father's murder. She felt more certain of it than ever. The question was how to prove it. She would not give up until she did—even if it meant risking her own life. Gareth must have thought that that man would scare her away—but the opposite was true. Gwen was not one to back down. And when someone tried to scare or threaten her, she always fought back twice as hard.

She turned yet another corner, and finally saw the tavern, crooked, sagging on one end, the structure way too old and never tended well to begin with. The door was partially open, and two drunks stumbled out of it, one of them lighting up at the sight of her.

"Hey, look here!" he said, elbowing his buddy, who, more drunk than he, turned and belched at her.

"Hey miss, going our way?" he yelled, and shrieked with laughter at his own joke.

They lurched towards her, but after what she had been through, Gwen was not afraid. She was in no mood for everyday cretins—and she pushed them roughly out of her way. Caught off guard, they stumbled back, drunk.

"Hey!" one screamed, indignant.

But Gwen hurried past them, unafraid, right into the open tavern. In the mood she was in, if one of them followed her in, she would find an empty glass and smash it on his head. That would make them think twice about addressing a member of the royal family so disrespectfully.

Gwen strode into the tavern, the smell hitting her, and as she did, the rowdy atmosphere fell silent, all heads turning. There were dozens of seedy types in here, all drinking, all slovenly; she could scarcely believe how many people were so deep into drink so early in the day. It was not a holiday, at least as far she could recall. Then again, she supposed that for these people, it always was.

One man, seated at the bar, was slower to turn than the others, and when he did, his eyes opened wide at the sight of her.

"Gwen!" he called out, surprise in his voice.

Gwen hurried over to Godfrey, feeling all the emotion pouring out of her. Godfrey looked at her with real concern, stumbled up from his barstool, and hurried over to her, laying a protective arm around her.

He guided her away from the others, to a small table in the corner of the tavern. His two friends, Akorth and Fulton, kept others at bay, and created a wall for their privacy.

"What happened?" he asked, quietly and urgently, as he sat beside her. "What happened to your face?" he asked, reaching towards her cut.

Her back to all the others, she sat beside her brother, and finally felt all her emotion pouring out. Despite her best efforts, she broke down sobbing, covering her face in her hands, in shame.

"Gareth tried to kill me," she said.

"What!?" Godfrey exclaimed, horrified.

"He sent one of his attack dogs after me. I was bathing, in King's River. He surprised me. I should have been more vigilant. I was stupid. I was caught off guard."

"Let me see," Godfrey said, pulling back her hand from her scar.

He looked at her cheek, then turned and snapped his fingers at Akorth, who ran off behind the bar and returned shortly with a clean, wet rag. He handed it to Godfrey, who wiped her cheek carefully and thoroughly. The cold water stung as he did, but she was grateful for his help. He handed her the rag and she held it to her cheek.

She saw his genuine concern, and for the first time in her life, she felt a real brotherly love for him, felt proud that Godfrey was her brother, felt that he was someone she could rely on. It broke her heart that he stayed in this place.

"Why are you here?" she asked. "I looked for you everywhere, and I was told that you'd come back here. You promised. You promised your drinking days were over."

Godfrey looked down at the table, crestfallen.

"I tried," he said, crushed. "I really did. But the pull of drink was too strong. After today, after our failure in the servant's quarters...I don't know. My hopes got so high. I was sure Steffen would give us the proof we needed. But after that failed, I lost hope. I got depressed. And then I heard the news of Kendrick, and that pushed me over the edge. I needed a drink. I'm sorry. I couldn't control it. I know I shouldn't have come back here. But I did."

"What news?" Gwen asked, alarmed. "What news of Kendrick?"

He looked at her, surprised.

"You haven't heard?"

She shook her head, welling with anxiety.

"Gareth had him arrested. He's been charged with our father's murder."

"What?" Gwen called out, horrified. "Gareth can't get away with that! That is ridiculous!"

Godfrey looked down and shook his head slowly.

"He already has. He is King—he can do whatever he wants now. It is heresy to question the King's judgment, isn't it? And worse: Kendrick is set to be executed."

Gwen felt a pit in her stomach. She didn't think she could feel any worse than she had this morning. But now she did. Kendrick, who she loved more than anything, imprisoned, set to be killed. It made her physically sick to think of it, to think of him, such a fine man, wallowing away in the dungeon, and executed like a common criminal.

"We must stop it," Gwen urged. "We can't allow him to die!"

"I agree," Godfrey said. "I can't believe Gareth tried to harm you," Godfrey said, looking really stunned.

"Can't you?" Gwen asked. "It seems he will stop at nothing until we're all dead. We're all obstacles, don't you see? We're all obstacles in his mind. He needs us out of the way. Because we know his true nature. He is guilty of our father's murder. And he won't stop until the rest of us are dead."

80

Godfrey sat there, shaking his head.

"I wish we could do more," Godfrey said. "We have to stop him."

"We both do," Gwen answered. "We can't wait any longer."

"I was thinking, this morning," Godfrey said, sitting up straight, eyes lighting with excitement, "of something that happened the other day. In the forest. I crossed paths with Gareth. He was with Firth. There is supposedly a witch's cottage not far from there. I'm wondering if that's where he was coming from. I was thinking of going to see if I could find this cottage. Perhaps I can discover something."

"You should go," Gwen answered. "It is a good idea. If not now, when?"

Godfrey nodded.

"But first, you need to stop all of this," she said, looking around the bar.

Godfrey looked into her eyes and he must have saw her meaning, as she looked around the tavern. She meant that it was time for him to stop his ways. To stop the drinking, once and for all.

Something shifted in his eyes as he looked at her, and she could almost see the transformation happening before her eyes. She could see his resolve. It seemed real this time.

"I will," he said, with a confidence unlike any she had ever heard. She felt it, and she really believed him.

"And I will go to our brother," Gwen said. "I will find a way to get to Kendrick in the dungeon, and I will find a way to get him out. Whatever I have to do. I cannot let him die."

Godfrey reached out and laid a hand on her wrist.

"Protect yourself," he urged, "Gareth will come after you again. You are the weakest link. You cannot walk around unprotected. Take this."

Gwen heard a clank, and looked down and saw him slide forward a small piece of wood on the table. She examined it, puzzled.

Godfrey reached over, and showed her the trick to it. He grabbed the wood and pried it open, an invisible crack down the middle, and both sides split in half, and there emerged a hidden dagger.

"It is the weapon of choice in the taverns," he explained. "Easy to hide. Untraceable."

Godfrey turned and looked at her meaningfully.

"Keep it close. And if anyone comes near you again, don't ask questions. Plunge it into their heart."

CHAPTER TWELVE

"On your feet!"

Thor opened his eyes with a jolt and looked up, disoriented, trying to figure out where he was. Several Legion commanders stood over him and the other boys, all of whom lay scattered on the ground, deep in sleep. Hands on their hips, the commanders prodded the boys with their feet, and Thor felt a boot in his side, and looked over to see Kolk prodding him. Krohn snarled in Thor's defense, and Kolk moved on to the next boy, screaming, taking his metal axe and slamming into his metal shield right above O'Connor's head. There was a resounding boom, and O'Connor leapt to his feet, eyes open wide.

Thor stood, too, rubbing his head, trying to process it all. They were all in a cave, that much he knew. With him were about a dozen other Legion members, all in his age range. His head was splitting, and he could see from the mute light entering the cave that it was the crack of dawn. He tried to remember.

It was all a blur. He recalled the night before, climbing the cliff, finally reaching the island, laying there. Eventually, the other boys had made it up, too, and they had all been rounded up by the commanders of the Legion, who told them to rest for the night and prepare for morning. They had broken them up into small groups, based on their ages, and Thor had splintered off with Reese, O'Connor, Elden and the twins, along with four other boys Thor didn't know. They had been directed towards small caves in the craggy mountainside of the desolate island. Night had fallen fast, and a thick fog settled in, so Thor couldn't see more of what lay in store out there.

They had all barely made it to the cave, dripping wet, freezing, as dark settled in. Someone had built a fire, and Thor remembered laying down beside it, and falling fast asleep.

The next thing he knew, he had been awakened.

Thor's stomach growled in the morning light, but he dared not say anything. He had slept in his clothes and boots, as did the others, and at least the fire had partially dried them out.

The commanders prodded one boy after another out the cave, and Thor felt himself being pushed from behind, and he stumbled out, into the strong light of the morning. The red mist still hung over the island, seemed to rise up from the island itself, but at least in the morning light Thor could see much more of this place. The island was even more eerie than he remembered—a desolate landscape of boulders and rocks, of small mountains and large craters. The horizon stretched forever and there were no trees anywhere in sight. Thor could hear the waves crashing, omnipresent, and knew that the ocean lay below, somewhere over the edge of the cliffs that demarcated the island in every direction. It was a fateful reminder that if one got too close to the edge, one would go hurling to one's death.

Thor could hardly imagine how they would train here. This island was so empty, and there looked to be no training ground in sight—no targets, no weapons, no armor, no horses.

His brothers in arms filtered out of the cave and stood with him in the morning light, all of them huddling around, squinting, raising their hands to block the sun. Kolk marched before them, as angry and intense as ever.

"Don't applaud yourselves just because you made it here," Kolk said. "You must all really think you're something special. Well, you're not."

Kolk paced.

"Being on this island is a privilege," he continued. "Your staying here is not a right. It is not a gift. You will stay here if—and only if—you earn it. Every moment of every day. And that begins with your getting permission to be here in the first place. Before your training can begin, you must win permission from the locals."

"The locals?" O'Connor asked.

"This island is inhabited by an ancient warrior tribe. The Kavos. They've lived and trained here a thousand years. Each and every warrior that comes here must ask and gain their permission. If you don't, you'll get shipped back to the Ring. You Legion members have been broken down into small groups, and you will each, separately, need to gain permission. You cannot count on the entire Legion now—only on the members in your group."

Thor looked around at his group of eight and wondered.

"But where are they?" Elden asked, rubbing his eyes against the morning sun. "The Kavos?"

"Finding them will not be easy," Kolk said. "They don't want to be found. They don't like you. And for many of you recruits, it will not go well. They are a belligerent people. They will challenge you. That is how your test of manhood begins."

"But how do we find them?" Conven pressed.

Kolk frowned.

"This island is vast and unforgiving. You may not ever find them. You may starve trying to get there. You may get lost. You may not make it back."

Kolk put his hands on his hips and smiled.

"Welcome to The Hundred."

*

Thor turned and looked at his group: there were eight of them, standing there, in the middle of nowhere, looking at each other, dazed and confused. Exhausted. There was O'Connor, Reese, Elden, the twins—and two others. One he recognized—the coward, the boy who froze up on the ships, who Thor rescued. And there was one other, whom Thor did not recognize. He looked to be their age, and he stood apart from the rest, with dark hair and eyes, looking away from the others, and with a permanent scowl on his face. There was something about him that Thor did not like, something that seemed dark. Something ... evil.

"So where now?" O'Connor asked.

The others grumbled and looked away.

"Where are the Kavos?" Elden asked.

Reese shrugged.

"I have no idea."

"Well, to the South is the ocean, so we can't go there," Reese said. "We can head North, East, or West. That wasteland he spokes of looks like it's to the north," he said, squinting into the horizon.

"This entire island looks like a wasteland," Elden said.

"I say we head north, and see what happens," Reese said.

The others all seemed to be in agreement, and they set off, beginning their long march. Krohn, whining, marched beside Thor.

"I'm William," said a boy, and Thor turned to see the boy he had saved in the waters, the one who had been afraid of the shield exercise. He walked beside Thor and looked at him gratefully. "I never had a chance to thank you for saving my life back there, in the sea."

"I'm Thor," he answered, "and you have nothing to thank me for."

Thor liked him; he was a frail, thin boy with large hazel eyes and longish hair that fell over his eyes. There was something to his demeanor that worried Thor—he seemed fragile. He didn't seem as strong as the others, and he seemed very on edge. Thor sensed that he wasn't cut out to be here.

Thor hiked silently with the seven other boys across the wasteland for hours, the only sound that of their boots crunching on rocks and dirt, each lost in his own world of anticipation. It was unusually cold for a summer morning, even as the first sun began to rise, and the mist still lingered, up to their ankles. A persistent cold breeze swept through this place that never seemed to go away. The eight of them walked in silence, side-by-side, marching with nothing but more wasteland on the horizon. Thor swallowed, thirsty, nervous, wondering if they would find wherever it was they needed to go—and not sure he wanted to. It had been much more reassuring having dozens of his Legion members around—and with just the eight of them, he felt more prone to attack.

Thor heard the distant screech of an animal, and it was unlike any animal noise he'd ever heard. It sounded like an eagle crossed with a bear. The others turned and looked, too, and Thor saw real fear in William's eyes. Thor looked around, trying to pinpoint where it was coming from, but it was impossible. There was nothing but wasteland, fading into the mist.

The others looked on edge—except for the final boy, the dark-haired one whose name, Thor remembered, was Malic. He still scowled, and he seemed preoccupied, lost in his own world. As Thor observed him, he began to dimly remember who he was. He remembered hearing rumors about him, the one boy who had joined the Legion by killing a man. If the rumors were true, they had come to his town for Selection and had skipped him over, and he rushed forward and killed a man twice his size in front of them. Impressed, they had decided to change their minds and accept him into the Legion. Apparently in every crop of the Legion, so Reese told him, they liked to take in one person who set everyone else on edge, who was a trained, ruthless killer. In this crop, that was Malic.

Thor looked away, and focused again on the landscape, on his surroundings, trying to stay vigilant. He looked up and realized there was a different hue to the sky, an orange green; there was a strange, thick feel to the mist, a different smell to the air, cool and crisp. This place was different than any place he'd ever been. Everything about it felt foreign. Whatever power he held within him was telling him something about this place, that it was different, primordial. He could feel the presence of the dragon, the force of its breath.

In fact, as they walked, he couldn't help but feel as if they were inside a dragon's lair, walking on the mist created by its breath. The place felt magical. It was like the feeling he'd had when crossing the Canyon—but it was different here. Here, it had a more ominous quality. Thor felt certain that other creatures lived here, too—and none that were welcoming.

"And what if when we find these Kavos they say no?" O'Connor called out to the group, wondering aloud the same thing that was on everyone's mind.

"What if they don't give us permission?" O'Connor continued. "Then what?"

"Then we *make* them give us permission," Elden answered. "If it is not given to us, then we fight for it. Do you think our enemies in battle will grant us permission to invade their towns? That's why we're here, isn't it? Isn't that what this is all about?"

Reese shrugged.

"I don't know what this is all about," he said. "All I know is that I remember the stories I heard from my older brother, Kendrick. He told me of the first time he came here. His close friends both died."

Thor felt a chill at his words. He turned and looked at Reese, and he could tell from his face that he was serious. The others looked more anxious than before.

"How?" O'Connor asked.

Reese shrugged.

"He wouldn't tell me."

"But do you really think they would let Legion members die here?" Conval asked.

"What purpose would that serve? To kill off their own recruits?" Conven added.

Reese shrugged, and fell silent as they all continued marching.

"You said it yourself. Recruits," Malic suddenly said.

Everyone turned to him, surprised. His voice was dark and guttural, surprising Thor, as he had never heard it before. He did not look back at them, but stared straight ahead, his hand always on the hilt of his dagger, playing with it as if it were his best friend. Its black-and-silver handle gleamed in the light.

"Recruits," he added. "We're all recruits. None of us are members. No one is truly a Legion member until they graduate. Age twenty. Six years to go. They're trying to weed us all out. They want a force of the most elite knights in the world. If we can't make it, they want us dead. They don't care.

Why should they? There are a thousand more just like us in every village in the Ring."

Thor thought about that as they fell back in silence and continued to march, their boots crunching. They headed deeper and deeper into the wilderness of this place, and Thor wondered about the other Legion members, all the other groups, where on the island they were, what obstacles they had to face. He was glad to be in the company of these boys.

As hours more passed, as the sun reached its peak in the sky, as Thor was fading out, beginning to lose focus, suddenly, there came a loud hissing and bubbling noise right near him. He jumped out of the way just in time, and beside him, the earth suddenly bubbled up. He watched the soil turn orange, then bright red, then hiss and explode. Lava shot up, high into the air, sparking and smoking, sending small flames in every direction. A small burst of flame landed on Thor's sleeve, and he swatted it as it began to burn him; luckily, he managed to put it out, although it lasted long enough to sting. Krohn snarled at it, ready to attack the lava.

Thor and the other boys ran away from the bursting lava spring, keeping their distance as it seemed to bubble ever higher. It was a good thing they did, because the ground around it began to melt.

"What is this place?" William asked, fear in his voice.

"Let's keep moving," Reese said.

They all turned and continued heading north, hurrying away from the lava burst. But just as they were gaining their distance, suddenly, another lava spring burst up from the ground, with no warning, just a few feet away on their other side.

William screamed and jumped, the flames just missing him.

They all hurried to gain distance from that one, too—but then, suddenly, all around them and as far as they could see, lava springs burst out. There came hissing and popping noises everywhere, as the land burst up like a minefield. Even while terrified, Thor could not help but notice that it created a beautiful display of light.

They all stood rooted in place, afraid to take a step forward. Lava springs were spaced out every twenty feet or so and it would be tricky to navigate between them.

"How are we supposed to continue through that?" William asked.

"At least they've already exploded," Elden said. "Now all we have to do is walk between them."

"But what if others explode?" William asked.

Clearly, they had no choice.

They all continued forward, into the lava field, Thor careful, with the others, to weave in between the lava springs. Luckily, no others burst as they went, but Thor was on guard the entire time.

Just as the lava field seemed to reach its end, suddenly, one last lava spring burst up, catching them all off guard. It burst right near O'Connor, too close for him to get out of the way in time. His screams filled the air, as did the stench of burning flesh. O'Connor's left bicep was singed badly by a glob of lava and O'Connor screamed, smoke and flames rising from his tunic. Standing right beside him was Malic, who could easily have helped him put it out. But he did not.

Thor and Reese jumped onto O'Connor, knocking him down, putting it out. O'Connor screamed, and Thor saw the burn was bad, and it looked incredibly painful.

He and Reese pulled O'Connor to his feet, and Thor tore a fresh piece of cloth from his own tunic, and wrapped it around O'Connor's arm.

"Why didn't you help him?" Reese yelled at Malic. "You were standing right beside him. You could have put it out."

Thor had been wondering the same thing.

Malic shrugged, nonchalant, then actually smiled over at them.

"Why should I?" he asked. "Why should I care if he gets burned?"

Thor stared back, disbelieving.

"Are you saying you don't care about protecting your brothers?" Elden asked.

Malic smiled back, and Thor could sense the evil in his eyes.

"Of course I don't. In fact, I would kill each one of you if I thought it benefited me."

His smile never disappeared, and Thor could see how serious he was. Just looking at him, seeing the depth of his evil, gave him a chill.

The others stared back at him, flabbergasted.

"We should all kill you right now," Elden answered.

"Then do it," Malic said. "Give me a reason to kill you."

Elden took a step towards him, scowling, drawing his sword—but suddenly, the twins stepped between them.

"Don't waste your time," Conven said to Elden. "He's not worth it."

Elden stopped, scowling, then finally turned away.

Krohn, beside Thor, clearly did not like Malic either. He growled quietly in his direction, the hairs standing up on his back whenever he looked at him.

"Let's get out of this place," Reese said. "Can you walk?" he asked O'Connor, who stood between them, breathing hard and clutching his arm.

O'Connor nodded back.

"It hurts like hell. But I'll be okay."

The group continued on, marching through the wasteland, all of them on edge, looking out for more lava springs. Finally, after an hour, Thor felt confident they'd passed them, and began to lower his guard.

As they walked and walked, as the sun grew longer in the sky, Thor began to wonder how long this would go on, and whether they would ever find the Kavos. How lost were they?

"How do we know we're even going in the right direction?" William suddenly called out to the group, echoing what was on everybody's minds.

He was met with only silence in return, and the whistling of the wind. That was answer enough—no one knew.

Hour followed hour as they marched through the wasteland, dirt and stones crunching beneath their feet. Thor was getting tired and hungry, and above all thirsty. The cool morning had morphed into a hot day, and the wind that whipped through only brought dust and more hot air. He licked his lips and realized he would do anything for a sack of water.

Thor looked up and blinked as he thought he spotted something scurrying in the distance. He'd thought it looked something like an ostrich, though it came and went so fast, he was unsure. Could it be? An animal in this place, in the middle of nowhere?

He squinted into the light, the morning mist now mostly burnt off, and thought he saw a small cloud of dust.

"Did you see that?" he asked Reese.

"What?" Reese said.

"I saw it," Conven said. "It looked like some kind of animal."

Now Thor wondered. As they all continued to march, suddenly, another animal sprinted right for them. They drew their swords, but the animal moved too quickly, and veered away at the last second.

"What the hell was that?" Conval asked.

Thor had definitely seen it this time—it had a bright yellow and black body, a round belly, long, skinny legs, at least ten feet high, with short, thick wings for arms, and a huge head. It looked like a bumblebee on stilts.

Suddenly, another one came darting out of nowhere, charging right for them. This one screeched as it went, flapping its wings with a buzzing noise, and seemed to charge right for Thor. Thor, his sword drawn, dodged out of the way at the last second, as the beast brushed by him. He swung his sword, but the beast was so fast, he wasn't even close. He swung at air. Krohn snarled and snapped at it, but also missed. He didn't know how something that big could move that fast. The brush with the beast left a bruise on his arm.

The others look baffled, but Reese nodded knowingly.

"Hemlocks," Reese said, relaxing his guard. "They're harmless, unless you provoke them."

"Harmless?" O'Connor said. "That didn't seem harmless."

"Provoke them like how?" Elden said. "You mean by, like, going into their territory? Because that is exactly what we are doing."

Thor studied the horizon and suddenly there came into view hundreds of hemlocks, scurrying every which way, their wings flapping and buzzing, gathering in the distance and making a great noise like a hornet's nest. They zigzagged left and right, and all eight boys stopped in their tracks. They stood there, frozen, unsure what to do. It was clear that if they continued to move forward, they'd be attacked.

"Backup slowly," Reese said. "Don't take your eyes off them. They'll take it as a sign of weakness."

They each backed up slowly, one step at a time, and after several minutes, they gained enough distance to be safely out of range.

"We can't continue in that direction," Conval said.

"Let's turn this way," Conven said.

They made a sharp turn to the right, taking a narrow trail between two mountains. As soon as they were safely out of sight, they broke into a jog, trying to put as much distance between them and the creatures as they could.

"You think they'll follow us?" O'Connor asked.

"I hope not," William said.

They jogged for what felt like an hour, until finally they came out the other side of the mountains, and found themselves in a new wasteland.

They switched to a walk, all breathing hard, Thor covered in sweat. The sun grew long in the afternoon, and Thor would give anything for a drink. He looked around and saw the others were as exhausted as he.

"This is stupid," William finally said. "How are we going to find them? We could be heading in the wrong direction."

"We just have to keep moving," Reese said.

"Moving where?" Elden asked, frustrated.

"Maybe this is all just an exercise," O'Connor said. "To get us all killed. Maybe these Kavos don't even exist. Maybe this whole thing was a test—to see how long and far we would go until we realized and turned back around. Maybe they're all waiting for us back where we began."

"That's ridiculous," Elden said. "We have our mission. We can't quit."

William stopped, and they all stopped and looked at him.

"I think we should turn around," he said.

"If you don't keep walking," Malic began, "then I'm going to—"

Before he could finish his words, suddenly there came the sound of footsteps on the desert floor.

Thor spun in time to see a dozen of the fiercest warriors he had ever seen, charging right for them. They wore all black, their muscular arms and legs open to the air, and large, red helmets. They were tall and broad, muscles bulging, and they carried swords and shields and all manner of deadly weapons. They let out a fierce battle cry

"I think we've found them," Malic said.

Clearly, these were the Kavos. They had come out of nowhere—and they did not seem pleased.

Thor and the others turned and faced them, but with hardly enough time to react. None of them drew their swords, all of them unsure whether to provoke them or try to make peace.

"We have come to ask your permission!" Reese yelled out, as they charged, trying to mollify them.

"Never!" their leader screamed back.

Thor and the others went to draw their weapons—but by now, it was too late.

The Kavos pounced on them. They moved faster than Thor could imagine, and Thor saw his brethren raising their swords and shields. There was a great clang of metal, as they blocked the blows.

Thor raised his own sword, blocking a blow just before it reached his shoulder. The blow was so strong and fierce, it sent him stumbling several feet. As he looked up, the Kavos brought down his sword again, and Thor blocked that too. But then the Kavos, a huge man with a long, wild beard and bald head, leaned back and kicked Thor hard in the chest. The blow sent him flying back several feet, the wind knocked out of him.

Krohn snarled and pounced on the warrior, and was able to drive him back and keep him away from attacking Thor while he was down.

The twins were knocked down, too, along with William, Reese and O'Connor. Elden, with his sheer strength, was able to go blow for blow, but even he was getting beaten back. Thor could not understand how the Kavos were so strong—and why they were so hostile. He had thought they would grant permission. Now he understood they needed to fight for it.

Thor rolled out of the way as a sword came down at him; the blade stuck in the dirt, and Thor used the opportunity to swing around and use his shield to strike him in the ribs. There came a gasp, and the man collapsed to his knees. Thor jumped to his feet and kicked the man, sending him to his back.

But Thor was then tackled from the side by another one, driven down to the ground. He landed with a crash, winded again, his facing driven into the dirt. He tried to spin, but the Kavos pinned him down, a man three times his size. The man went to claw Thor's face, and Thor reached up to hold him back. But the man was too strong. Thor rolled his head out of the way, and at the last second the man's fingers flew by him and plunged into the dirt.

Thor tried to roll the man off him, but he was too strong. They rolled, several times, and the man stayed on top of him, pinning him down. The man reached up and Thor saw that he held a curved dagger and was brining it down for his face. There was nothing he could do about it. He braced himself for the impact.

Krohn appeared, snarling, and bit the man in the side of the head; he screamed and let go of Thor. Then Elden appeared, kicking the Kavos hard in his temple, the blow knocking him off. Thor jumped to his feet, beside Elden, more grateful to Krohn and to Elden than they would ever know.

"I owe you one," he said.

More of them charged, and they both spun and raised their swords and blocked the blows. Thor parried, back and forth, swords clanging, driven back and barely able to hold his own. These men were just too strong, too fast. They couldn't hold them back much longer.

Thor, desperate, was beginning to feel a power, an energy, welling within him. He felt a tremendous heat rise up, through his legs and arms and shoulders, into his palms. Suddenly his sword was knocked out of his hand, and he found himself defenseless. The Kavos reached back to swing, and as he did, Thor felt his palms positively burning. He had to trust his instincts. He planted his feet, held a palm out, and directed his energy at the man.

As he did, he watched in awe as a golden ball of energy came flying out of his hands and hit the Kavos square in the chest. He went flying back, a good twenty feet, with a scream, and landed on his back. He lay there, unconscious.

The others must have noticed, because they all turned and looked at Thor, stunned. Thor held out his palms, aiming them at one Kavos after the next. One after another, a golden energy ball came flying out, hitting each Kavos, knocking each one onto his back. He first hit the one attacking Reese, then Elden, then O'Connor, then the others. He saved each one, sparing each a nasty blow from his attacker.

There was one Kavos, larger than the others, with a different colored armor, who looked like their leader. He charged Thor, and Thor turned and fired an energy ball at him.

But Thor was shocked to see the man swipe it away before it reached him.

The man took three steps to Thor, grabbed him by the shirt, and hoisted him up high in the air, several feet, until he was eye level with him. He held them there, staring at him, scowling.

Thor felt a tremendous energy flowing through the man, and realized, whoever he was, he was helpless in his grasp. If this man wanted to kill him, Thor knew that he could.

As the man held Thor in the air, after several seconds, slowly his expression softened, and to Thor's surprise, it morphed into a smile.

"I like you," the man growled, in a deep, ancient voice. "I wish to have you here."

He leaned back, and threw Thor and he went flying through the air, landing hard in the dirt, rolling several times, winded again. He lay there, breathing hard, and looked up at the warrior.

The man laughed, then turned his back, and began to walk away.

"Welcome to the Isle of Mist," he said.

CHAPTER THIRTEEN

Erec woke at dawn in the unfamiliar bed and sat upright, trying to get his bearings. He remembered: he was in the tavern. Alistair.

He jumped up and dressed himself within moments, preparing. He had been up most of the night, barely sleeping, the blood pumping in his veins with thoughts of Alistair. He could not get her face from his mind, and he could barely stand the thought that she was sleeping just down the hall, under the same roof. He also could not rest knowing she had not yet agreed to accept his proposal.

As he put on his chainmail, as he watched the first light breaking through the crooked window, he knew that today was the day. Today was the day his new life would begin, the first day of one hundred days of tournaments to win his bride. Now he had a reason to win. If she would have him, he would fight for her.

As Erec watched the sun slowly light up the world, the trees in silhouette, as he heard the first birds sing, he was struck with a feeling, one he could not shake: if she said yes, today was the day that would change his life. His entire life, when he had met women, he had never had such a feeling as when he had met Alistair. When he had found her again, in the tavern, he had been expecting not to feel that same feeling again. He had been surprised to realize that he felt it still—and even stronger. It was not a fluke. It was a feeling of instant loyalty to her. A feeling that he could be by no one else's side. He did not know if she felt it, too. And he could not tell if that was because she was overwhelmed, or because she was simply not interested. He had to know. He could not rest until he did.

Erec finished dressing, gathered his weapons, and hurried from the room, his spurs jingling as his footsteps echoed down the creaky wooden hall. He hurried down the steps, entered the tavern, empty save for him, all the others still sleeping. He sat at one of the empty tables, waiting. Hoping. Was she awake? He wondered. Would she even care?

Moments later, the kitchen door opened and the innkeeper stuck out his head, looked disapprovingly at Erec, then closed the door quickly. There followed a yelling, a clattering of pots behind the closed door, and moments later, the door opened, and she appeared.

The sight of her took his breath away. She wore the same clothes from the night before, her hair was disheveled, and he could see she had been hastily awakened. She also looked tired, as if she had not slept much. Nonetheless, she looked as beautiful to him as ever. Her large blue eyes glowed in the morning light, emanating a power unlike any he had encountered.

Alistair hurried to his table, holding a mug of ale, her head lowered in humility, and set it down before him, still not meeting his eyes. He wanted more than anything to look into those eyes, to know how she felt about him. He was about to speak to her, when suddenly the innkeeper appeared behind her, hurrying up to her. Alistair became nervous, and she bumped the table, and a little bit of ale spilled out onto the floor.

"Look what you've done!" the innkeeper screamed at her. "Filthy, stupid girl! Mop it up!"

Erec reddened at his harsh words, his rage rising.

Alistair spun, nervous, and as she did, by accident she swiped the glass, which went sliding across the table and landed on the floor with a crash. The glass shattered, and the liquid went everywhere.

"Stupid wench!" the innkeeper screamed. He pulled back his large open palm, and brought it down for her face.

But Erec was faster than he. Erec drew on his soldier's reflexes and leapt up from the bench and caught the innkeeper's hand in mid-swing. He caught his wrist firmly, right before he hit Alistair, and held it in place.

The man glowered down at him, but Erec was stronger, and with one hand he bent his wrist back, turning it until the innkeeper dropped to his knees.

"If you ever try to lay a hand on her again," Erec said, as he extracted a dagger and held it at the base of the innkeeper's throat, "I swear to God I will kill you."

The innkeeper swallowed, his eyes open wide with fear.

"My lord, please don't hurt him," Alistair said softly.

Erec was mollified by the sound of her voice, and he softened just a little, especially as the innkeeper gulped, and sweat broke out on his forehead.

"I won't touch her," the innkeeper said, his voice raspy from the tip of the blade. "I promise."

Erec let him go, and the innkeeper dropped his arm and rubbed his wrist, breathing hard.

"Will you join me?" he asked Alistair, gesturing at the seat opposite him at the table.

"She has to work!" the innkeeper yelled back, as he got to his feet.

"If I win the tournaments, and if she agrees, then she will be my bride," Erec said to the innkeeper. "She will never have to work again."

"She might be your bride," the innkeeper snapped, "but just because she is married, that doesn't absolve her of me. She's an indentured servant to me. She has four more years on her contract."

Erec looked at Alistair, and she looked at him and nodded, her eyes wet.

"It is true, my lord. You see, I am not such a good bride for you. I am indentured here. I must repay my debt before I am free to go."

Erec turned and scowled at this innkeeper. He hated him with a loathing he did not think possible.

"And how much is her contract worth?" Erec asked.

"That's no business of yours—"

"Answer me!" Erec growled, putting one hand on his dagger.

The innkeeper must have detected Erec's seriousness, because he swallowed and looked back.

"The typical servant is paid room and board and 100 pence for a seven year contract," he said.

"If I win the jousting, and if she agrees to be my bride, I will buy her contract from you. In fact, I will pay you triple."

Erec took a sack of gold coins from his waist, and dropped it on the table. It landed with a clang.

"300 pence of the king's gold," Erec announced.

The innkeeper looked down, wide-eyed. He licked his lips in greed, looking from Erec to Alistair. Then he grabbed the sack, weighed it in his palm, and opened it, examining the contents.

Finally, he stuffed the sack into his pocket. He shrugged.

"Take her then," he said. "It is your money to lose. Only a fool would throw away so much gold for a servant."

"Please, my Lord, don't do this," Alistair cried out to Erec. "It is too much money! I am not worth it!"

The innkeeper was about to go, but stopped and turned.

"And if you don't win the competition? And if she doesn't agree to be your bride?" he asked.

"As long as she is set free," Erec said, "the gold is yours to keep."

The innkeeper smiled, turned, and hurried from the room, slamming the kitchen door behind him.

Finally, it was just Erec and Alistair, alone in the room.

Erec Turned and looked at her.

"Do you wish to marry me?" he asked her, with more seriousness than he had ever mustered.

Alistair lowered her head in humility, and Erec's heart pounded as he awaited her response. What if she said no?

"My lord," she said. "I could think of no greater honor, no greater dream for any maiden in the kingdom than to be your wife. But I do not deserve this. I am but a common servant girl. You would sully your great name to be with me."

Erec's heart swelled with love for her, and he knew at that moment that he did not care what others thought—he wanted to spend the rest of his life with her.

"Will you marry me?" he asked her directly.

She lowered her head, and Erec stepped forward, placed a hand gently on her chin, and raised it.

She looked up at him, and her eyes were filled with tears.

"You cry," he said, crushed. "That is a no."

She shook her head.

"They are tears of joy, my lord," she said. "From the moment I laid eyes on you, I wanted nothing else," she said. "My heart was too overwhelmed to say it. I dared not to dream."

They embraced, and he held her tight in a hug. The feel of her body enwrapped in his was greater than anything he had felt in his life.

"Please, my lord," she whispered into his ear. "Win this jousting. Win it for me."

CHAPTER FOURTEEN

Thor, drenched in sweat, stood with the other boys in the Legion, trying to catch his breath. The second sun was at its peak, beating down on him overhead, and it had been a relentless day already.

After gaining permission from the Kavos and finally finding their way back to the other Legion members the night before, they had all crashed on the desert floor. It felt to Thor as if he had just closed his eyes when he had been awakened early, at the crack of dawn of another day—and since then, they had not stopped training all day long.

It was the first day of training of The Hundred, and it was more grueling than anything he could imagine. They had been sparring since the morning, breaking off into groups with all different ages. They practiced throwing spears at moving targets; clanging shields for hours; sparring with extra-heavy swords; jumping over ravines; and wrestling with each other. As he turned and looked around, he saw that all the boys looked exhausted. It was as if they had crammed a week's worth of training into a morning, without a rest between. Every muscle in his body ached. He could not imagine how they could possibly keep up this pace for a hundred days. Maybe that was the point.

Finally, the commanders had summoned them all together, and he stood there with the others, catching his breath and staring back at Kolk, who paced among them.

"We have brought you to this island for a reason," he boomed. "Training here is different than anywhere in the world. If we wanted to engage you in technical exercises, we would have kept you back in the Ring. Here, there are unique aspects to training, to becoming a warrior, which you will learn nowhere else in the world. This island is known as a training ground to the elite warriors of every kingdom—not just the Ring. They come here from all corners of the globe to train, to learn techniques from each other, to spar with each other. And now it is time to expose you to the best of the best.

"IN FORMATION!" Kolk screamed.

The boys fell into rows of two, side-by-side, Thor standing next to Reese, and began marching up the steep hill, Krohn walking beside them. Thor looked up and saw that this hill seemed to climb right into the sky, the sun beating into his eyes. He could hardly believe they were marching to the top. Even reaching the plateau they had been sparring on had taken hours; to reach the top of this mountain would likely take them hours more.

Reese huffed beside him, out of breath.

"You know not everyone comes back," said Malic. He was speaking to William who marched beside him. Thor could see the terror in William's eyes, and he guessed Malic's point was to scare him. Malic must have sensed that William was more sensitive than the others, and it seemed he wanted to break him. Thor did not understand what Malic's problem was. Did he hate everyone? Or was he born evil?

"What do you mean?" William asked, fearful.

"There's a quota, you know," Malic said. "To the Legion. Even if we do well, they have to leave some of us behind."

"That's not true," Reese said.

"That's what I heard," Malic said.

"Not everyone makes the Legion," Elden corrected, turning around. "But that's not because there's a quota. That's because they fail out. It's based on performance."

"They wouldn't leave us here, behind on this island, would they?" William asked, fear in his voice.

"Of course they would," Malic answered.

William looked at his surroundings with a new sense of fear. There came an awful squawking noise, and they looked up as a huge bird swooped down low and circled over them. It looked like a buzzard, but had three heads and a long yellow tail. It seemed to stare right at William. It squawked again and raised its tail.

"What's that?" William asked.

"A galtross," Reese said. "A scavenger."

"They say it singles out the walking dead," Malic added. "Whoever it follows will die next."

It squawked right at William, and Thor could see him overcome by fear.

"Why don't you leave him alone?" Thor said to Malic.

"I will treat him anyway I wish," Malic said. "And when I'm finished, I'll turn to you."

Thor watched Malic's hand slip down and rest on his belt, on his dagger.

Krohn snarled at Malic.

"Try anything against my friend, and it will be my knife you feel in your back," Reese said to Malic.

"And mine," O'Connor added.

But Malic, unfazed, only smiled. He actually let out a laugh as he turned back and continued to march.

"The Hundred is long," he said ominously, then fell silent.

The group, filled with a tense silence, continued to march.

The incline of the mountain became more steep, and soon they hand to nearly get down on their hands and knees and crawl their way up.

After what felt like hours, Thor's legs burning, finally, they reached a wide plateau at the very top of the mountain. All the boys collapsed, Thor among them.

They lay there, breathing hard, engulfed in an actual cloud. It was impossible to see anything, enveloped in the mist. Thor lay there, gasping for air, more tired than he ever thought possible.

"ON YOUR FEET!" came a scream.

Somehow, Thor forced himself to his feet with all the other boys, and as they did, the cloud lifted. Thor was shocked to see, standing there, a large group of disparate warriors. At their head was the fiercest looking warrior Thor had ever seen. His skin was a light green, his head was bald, he was three times the size of any man, he wore no shirt and short pants, and his muscles bulged. He had three scars across his chest and was missing one eye, and on his weapons belt hung nearly every manner of weapon. He was a one-man army.

Behind him stood a dozen warriors, of all different sizes and races and shapes. They were the most exotic looking warriors Thor had ever seen, and he could tell they had come from countries far and wide outside the Ring. He was breathless. Real warriors. These men were his heroes. He had never met anyone from outside the Ring, much less other warriors.

"This is Kibotu," Kolk announced. "He is the resident trainer on this island. Warriors seek him out from all corners of the globe. He has trained the very best, and he is among the very best himself."

Kibotu gave Kolk a brief nod of respect, then looked over the Legion members. Thor felt as if he were staring right through him, and felt inadequate in his presence.

"Every year they bring to us a new crop of young warriors. Every year some of you make it, and some of you don't. A warrior's heart is strong. His spirit is stronger. This island is here to teach you the spirit of a warrior. It is an unforgiving place. Make no mistakes. Respect it, and it will respect you."

Thor looked over Kibotu's shoulder, and beyond him he could make out a training ground. There were various structures, vast sparring grounds, and dozens of warriors hard at work, training with every weapon imaginable. He watched warriors shooting bows and arrows into targets, hurling spears, attacking dummies with swords, and charging each other with lances. This place was alive with the warrior's spirit.

"You will train with us here today, and every day, until your Hundred is finished, until your spirits are worthy. Waste no time. Get into place!"

The boys looked at each other, puzzled.

"Break into your groups of eight!" Kolk commanded. "You know who you are. You will each take up a skill, and you will not stop until I say so!"

The Legion broke off and ran over to the training ground, and Thor was directed by the commanders, along with his group of eight, to the spear-hurling ground at the far end.

Thor stood there and waited his turn as one after the other, the seven boys grabbed a spear, one at a time, and aimed for a distant target—a piece of wood cut into the shape of a circle and nailed to a tree. One by one, they each missed. The target was just too far, and too small. They all fell short.

It was Thor's turn. He lifted the long, bronze spear, longer and heavier than any spear he had ever held. He aimed for the target. But the target was so far away, farther than any target he had ever aimed for, he could not imagine how he would hit it.

He took three steps and hurled it. He was embarrassed to watch it fall short, landing in the dirt by several feet.

"You throw with your body," came a harsh voice, "not your mind!"

Thor turned to see Kibotu himself standing over him, frowning down.

Kibotu stepped forward, grabbed a spear as if it were a toothpick, took one step, and hurled it. It soared through the air with lightning speed, and struck right in the middle of the bull's-eye.

Thor could not believe it. He felt like a boy next to this warrior. He wondered why Kibotu had singled him out, of all the boys.

"How did you do that?" he asked.

"I did not do that," Kibotu answered harshly. "The spear did that. That is your problem. You live with a separation between you and your weapon. You and the weapon must be one."

Kibotu thrust another spear into Thor's hand, yanked his shoulder back, turned his neck and positioned it to face the bull's-eye.

"Close your eyes," he commanded.

Thor did so.

"When you step forward, see in your mind's eye the spear entering the target. Do not release the spear. Let it release you."

Thor focused, and felt the spear in a way he never had before. He felt a tremendous energy coursing through his system. He breathed deep.

He opened his eyes and took several steps and hurled it, and this time it felt different as he released it. It felt lighter. It felt perfect.

Thor did not even need to look to know the result. He felt it. He saw what he already knew: it was a perfect bull's eye. It was the only throw of all the boys to even hit the target.

Thor turned and smiled up at Kibotu, expecting praise.

But to his surprise, Kibotu had already turned and walked away. Thor did not know if that meant he was satisfied, or disappointed. And he still didn't know why he had singled him out.

The exercises continued all day long, going from one skill to the next, until finally a horn sounded, and pandemonium broke out. Before Thor could grasp what was happening, boys were crisscrossing the training ground in every direction, and he suddenly saw Malic, charging right for him, a dagger in his hand. Malic scowled, and Thor could see on his face the intent to kill, and he lunged at Thor, about to thrust the dagger into his heart.

It all happened too quickly—Thor could not react in time. He braced himself, as he knew he was about to be killed.

Suddenly Krohn appeared, leaping into the air and digging his fangs into Malic's chest; Malic stumbled back, caught off guard, trying to get him off.

Before Thor could react, he suddenly felt himself tackled and pinned down to the ground from behind, his face planted in the soil.

Thor tried to get up, to figure out what was happening, as all around him others were hitting the ground, too. He spun around and realized there was someone on top of him. It was an exotic warrior, one he had never met, from a faraway kingdom. He was trying to pin him down.

It was then that Thor realized the sound of that horn meant that the training grounds were being opened up to wrestling. But then why had Malic attacked him with a knife? None of the others were using weapons.

Thor had never been taught how to wrestle, and he felt a searing pain in his shoulder as this warrior, a young warrior, maybe eighteen, with dark brown skin, large yellow eyes, a bald head and a scar running above his eyebrow, twisted him around and put one arm behind his back. He was stronger than Thor could ever dream, and Thor felt like his arm would snap.

He squirmed and struggled, and could not break free of this man's grip.

"YIELD!" yelled the warrior.

But Thor did not want to yield so quickly.

Just as Thor thought his arm couldn't bend anymore, just when he thought it was about to break, he heard a running noise, followed by a kick, and felt the warrior go flying off him.

Thor looked up, wanting to thank whoever it was—but was confused as he blinked into the sun to see that it was Malic.

Malic had freed himself from Krohn's grasp and then had kicked the warrior hard in the back of his head with his boot while he was on the ground, then he extracted a dagger, jumped down, and as the warrior turned, he stabbed him in the heart.

The warrior let out a horrified gasp, blood pouring out from his chest, all over the dagger. Thor sat there, horrified, hardly believing what was happening. He felt terrible: it had all happened too fast for him to react. Clearly, weapons were not supposed to be used in this training session. So why had Malic killed the man?

Before Thor could process it, Malic rushed to him, thrust the bloody weapon into his palm, then took off.

Another horn sounded, and suddenly Thor was surrounded by dozens of warriors, scowling down at him. Kibotu and Kolk walked over, and the other warriors cleared a path.

"What have you done?" Kibtou shouted down. "You have murdered one of my warriors! In a training session!"

"I killed no one!" Thor protested, looking down at the bloody dagger in his hand, and throwing it down to the soil. "I did not do this!"

"Then why do you hold the weapon?" Kibotu shouted.

"Malic did it!" Thor yelled.

There was a gasp, as the others turned and looked at Malic.

He appeared, being dragged by two warriors. Thor gained his feet, as more and more warriors gathered around, and he felt them all staring at him.

"I did not kill this man!" Malic lied. "I saw Thor do it. After all, that is his dagger. He was attacked by that man."

"Do you deny that you were attacked by that man?" Kibotu pressed Thor.

"He did attack me. We were wrestling. He was about to break my arm."

"So you admit you stabbed him," Kibotu said.

"No! I did not. I swear to you."

"Then I ask again: why do you hold the weapon?"

One of the warriors stepped forward and snatched the dagger from Thor's hand and handed it to Kibotu. Kibotu examined it, then handed it to Kolk.

Kolk held it up to the light, inspecting it. He nodded grimly.

"This is Thor's dagger," he confirmed.

"But I did not kill him!" Thor pleaded. "Malic planted it!"

Kibotu looked back and forth between Thor and Malic.

"One of you is lying. Only the fates will know. The murderer must be punished. On this island there is a belief that the Cyclops is the determiner of all things. Whoever faces the Cyclops, and lives, he is the one who is innocent. Whoever dies by his hand, the fates hold guilty."

Kibotu stepped forward and sighed.

"The two of you will fight the Cyclops. Whoever lives, he is innocent. Whoever dies, so be it. Blood must have blood."

Thor gulped. The Cyclops? He could not imagine facing such a monster, even though he was innocent. He felt himself grabbed roughly from behind, and bound with rope, digging into his wrists. Malic was, too. They were shoved from behind, and the group of warriors followed as they were led across the plateau, and down the steep mountain. Krohn marched beside Thor, whining, refusing to leave his side.

As they went, the second sun beginning to set, Thor could see the island spread out below him. From this vantage point, the sky was covered in beautiful shades of crimson and violet. Below him, far below, at the base of the mountain, lay dozens of caves.

He heard an earth-shattering roar, felt the ground shake beneath him, and he knew, with a sinking feeling, that he was being lead right into the monster's den.

CHAPTER FIFTEEN

Gwendolyn hurried through the castle corridors, on edge, beside herself with worry, having been unable to think of anything else since she heard of Kendrick's imprisonment and pending execution. Gareth had gone too far. She could not sit idly by. She felt so helpless; there had to be something she could do, some way she could help—and she would find out.

Gwen descended down the spiral stone staircase, deeper and deeper, into the bowels of the castle. She passed even the servants' level, and after several more levels, finally she reached a large, iron door. She wasted no time: she hurried up to it and pounded on it with her fists.

She waited breathlessly, her heart pounding, and finally several guards opened it. One held up a torch in the darkness.

"My lady," said the guard standing in the center.

"Is that the king's daughter?" another asked.

"The former king," another corrected.

"The current and always king," she corrected sternly, stepping forward. "It is I."

"What are you doing down here?" one asked, eyes wide. "This is no place for a lady."

"I need to see my brother. Kendrick."

The guards looked at each other, flustered.

"I'm sorry my lady, but Kendrick is to have no visitors. Under strict orders of the King."

Gwendolyn stared back at the guard firmly. She was determined, and she felt a strength overcoming her. The strength of her father.

"Look at my face," she said. "You have known me since I was a child. I have known you my entire life to be a faithful and obedient servant to my father."

The lead guard's face, lined with wrinkles, softened.

"That is true, my lady."

"Do you think my father would have prevented me from seeing my own brother, Kendrick?"

He blinked, thinking.

"Your father would have prevented you nothing," he said. "He had infinite space in his heart for you. His standing order was always that Gwendolyn gets whatever she wants."

Gwen nodded.

"So there you are," she said. "Now let me through."

"However," the guard said, blocking her way. "I also doubt your father would want his murderer to have any visitors."

Gwen fumed.

"Shame on you," she said firmly. "You've known Kendrick longer than I. You know there was no one who loved my father more. Do you honestly believe he had a hand it?"

The guard stared back, and she could see him thinking. Finally, his face gave in.

"No," he said softly. "I do not."

"Enough said," she said. "Now step aside and let me in. Enough with this nonsense. I'm here to see my brother, and see him I will," she said with a strength in her voice that surprised even her. It was a command—and it left no room for doubt.

The guard vacillated only for a moment, then finally motioned to the other guards, bowed his head and stepped aside. He opened the door wide, and as Gwen hurried passed, slammed it behind her.

"Follow me, and be quick about it my lady," he urged. "This place has many spies. I cannot let you down here for long. If I am caught, it will be myself in this dungeon."

Gwen followed him as he hurried down the corridor, their footsteps echoing in this place, dimly lit by torches, passing cell after cell. She saw prisoners in the shadows, sticking their faces into the bars of their cells, faces that had been down here too long. They were evil, lecherous faces, and some of them hissed at her as she passed. She doubled her speed, trying not to look too closely.

Finally, after turning down several more corridors, the guard led her to a single cell, the last one on the left. He stood behind her, waiting.

"Leave us," Gwen commanded.

The guard looked at her, hesitated a moment, then turned and left, leaving her alone.

Gwen looked through the cell, her heart pounding in anticipation, and stepped closer. Finally, Kendrick appeared, looking too pale, and smiling at the sight of her.

"My sister," he said.

He reached up and grabbed her hand through the bars.

She smiled back, as his face lit up, and it felt so good to see him, to see that he was alive, that he was okay. Her heart broke at the sight of him, at the indignity of Kendrick being in this place. He had been treated unfairly. And yet still he wore his kind, noble, compassionate smile. He was the finest man she knew.

"My sister," he repeated. "You do me a great service to come here."

"The service is to myself," she replied. "It is an honor to see you. I'm sorry I've not come sooner."

"I'm amazed you were able to come at all," he said, clasping her hand in both of his. His voice was weak and raspy, and she reached into her shirt and pulled out treats she hid for him. She slid it between the bars, and he looked down in wonder.

"Dried venison," she said. "Your favorite. Enough to give you strength."

He grabbed it and immediately took a bite, tearing the meat off the stick. He gulped it down, starving.

Gwen reached into her pocket and extracted a sack of water, and he drank. Then she reached into her waist and grabbed a pouch.

"I wanted you to have something sweet," she said, smiling. "Honey cakes. I pressed them myself."

She handed him the pouch, and his eyes welled with tears.

"You do our father a great honor," he said. "You know that I did not kill him, don't you?" he asked desperately.

She nodded.

"Of course. Or else I would not be here."

He nodded back. The sight of him down here nearly brought tears to her eyes; it made her madder at Gareth than ever. She burned at the unfairness of it all.

"Gareth considers us a threat," she said. "That is why you are here."

Kendrick stared back.

"That has always been his nature," he said. "His entire life's ambition has been our father's throne. And why would he feel threatened by everyone around him, unless he himself had a hand in the murder?"

Gwen stared back meaningfully.

"I've been thinking the same thoughts," she said. "After all, who else stands to gain?"

"But you must prove it. You must find the murder weapon," Kendrick said. "The dagger used to kill him. The one that is missing. That will be the key."

"Have you any idea where to look?" she asked.

Disappointingly, he shook his head.

"Gareth probably disposed of it, or had it disposed of," he answered. "And without it, it will be very hard to prove anything. It is all circumstantial. And until they prove anything, I may be down here until my execution."

It broke Gwen's heart to think of it, and she felt a chill race through her body.

"I will not allow it!" Gwen cried out. "I will find a way to stop him. I promise you. I will."

Kendrick shook his head.

"I wish I shared your optimism, but you are up against forces greater than you can imagine. There is

125

a conspiracy to cover up the death of our father, and its tentacles, I am sure, reach deep. Be careful in how you tread. Do not underestimate Gareth's villainy. Remember, you are up against the dragon?"

"The dragon?" Gwen asked.

"There are many types of dragons in this world. The evil of men's smiles can be more insidious than the fiercest dragon in the wild."

Gwen sighed, thinking about that. She knew he was right.

"There must be some way, someone who can help us get you out of here," she said.

As he stood there, shaking his head, suddenly, she had a flash of inspiration.

"Mother," she said, dreading it even as she spoke the words. If there was anyone she hated more than Gareth, it was her mother, and the one good thing that had come from her father's death was her mother's catatonic state, her leaving her alone. She had vowed to never see her again, and the idea of talking to her made her feel physically ill. But for Kendrick, she would do it.

"I don't know how she could help," Kendrick said. "She has been unable to speak since the death of our father. And even if she were, Gareth is king now. She is no longer queen. Her remaining influence, if any, is finite."

"But she was queen only days ago," Gwen countered. "Many people still answer to her, still fear and respect her and will defer to her wishes—especially those loyal to our father."

Kendrick nodded back.

"I concede there is a chance," he said.

He reached out, and grabbed both of her hands in his.

"Whatever happens, I want you to know that our father was right to choose you as the next ruler. I didn't see it before, but I see it now. He had been right all along."

Gwen looked back to him, her heart welling with gratitude.

"Also know that I love you," he said.

"I love you, too," she said, her eyes welling up. "Know that I will not let you die in here. I will allow myself to die first."

CHAPTER SIXTEEN

Thor descended down the mountain for the caves of the Cyclops, the sunset sky breaking all around him, lighting the world in a million shades of scarlet, and he felt as if he were being marched to his death—as if he were descending into hell itself.

He marched, the Legion members a safe distance behind him, Malic beside him, both of them still bound, Krohn to his side, the shouts of the beast, concealed in the cave, growing louder. The earth trembled as they went, and Thor could only imagine the ire of this beast.

Thor hated Malic with a passion reserved for no other. He had been unfairly setup because of him, unfairly accused, dragged into this, his potential death. Thor only prayed that the legend of the Cyclops held true—and that only the guilty one would be killed.

Thor thought back to that scene on the sparring field, and he remembered Malic's trying to kill him first. He still didn't really understand what had happened, or why.

"Before we are sent to our deaths," Thor said to Malic, walking side by side, "tell me one thing. Why did you do it? Why did you try to kill me back there? And when you failed, why did you then kill that man?"

Malic continued walking, and, to Thor's surprise, even as he was being marched to his death, he smiled, as if he enjoyed this. This boy was truly sick.

"I never liked you," Malic said. "From the moment I met you. But that was not the reason. I was paid handsomely for it—to kill you."

Thor was aghast.

"Paid?" he asked.

"You have very rich enemies. I gladly took their fee for attempting something I wanted to do myself."

"Then why did you kill that man I was wrestling with?" Thor asked. "What has he to do with me?"

"When I missed my chance to kill you," Malic said, "I figured my next best chance was to kill him and pin it on you. Then the warriors would kill you, and save me the trouble."

Thor frowned.

"Well it didn't work out that way, did it?" Thor asked.

"You will die by the Cyclops hand," Malic said.

"But so will you," Thor countered.

Malic shrugged.

"Everybody has to die sometime," he said, then fell into silence.

Thor could not understand him—he truly seemed apathetic to life. He wondered what evil had befallen him to make him this way.

"Just tell me one more thing before your death," Thor urged. "Who paid you? Who are my enemies?"

Malic continued walking, silent. Clearly, he was done speaking.

"Well," Thor concluded, "I hope you're satisfied. Now you're going to get us both killed."

"Wrong," Malic said. "I don't believe in legends and fairytales. The monster won't kill me. I am stronger than any monster. It will only kill one of us. And it will be you."

Thor looked at him with a hatred beyond calculation.

"I would kill you right now, if I could," Thor said.

Malic smiled.

"Then too bad we are both bound."

They continued marching, silently, getting ever closer, the sky turning darker, and the monster's roars growing louder.

"I like you," Malic said, surprising Thor. "In another life, we would be friends."

Thor looked at him, unbelieving.

"You are sick," Thor said. "I don't understand you. You said you hated me. We would never be friends. I am not friends with liars—or murderers."

Malic threw his head back and laughed loudly.

"Lying and murdering is the way of the world," he answered. "At least I am bold enough to admit it. Everyone else hides and cowers behind a façade."

The two of them continued marching, farther and farther down the hill, getting closer to the cave of the Cyclops. The sky morphed into a brilliant, glowing red, looking as if it were on fire. Thor could not help but feel as if he were walking into the very pit of hell.

Finally, the ground leveled out, the cave hardly thirty yards before them, and they stopped as two warriors came up behind them and cut their ropes, freeing their hands. The warriors turned and ran back uphill, to the large crowd of Legion members who watched at a safe distance uphill.

Thor and Malic glanced at each other, then Thor turned and marched boldly right up to the huge cave. Malic followed. If Thor was going to die, he would do so bravely. Krohn walked beside him, growling.

"Go back, Krohn!" Thor commanded, wanting to spare him.

But Krohn refused to leave his side.

There came another earth-shattering roar, and it was enough to make Thor want to stop in his tracks. Beside him, Malic continued marching, relaxed, with a smile on his face, as if happy to meet the monster. Maybe he was happy to meet his death, Thor thought. He seemed suicidal.

Thor's mind raced as they approached the cave. The opening was so high, soaring at least thirty feet, it was ominous; it made Thor wonder about the size of the creature that lived within it. He wondered if these would be his last moments on earth, if he would die this way, down here, in this cave, on this island. All because of Malic, because of a crime he did not commit. He wondered about his fate and destiny, if it had all been wrong. After all, Argon had never seen this, had never seen his encounter with the Cyclops—or at least had never warned him of it. And Thor had never seen it himself. Was his power not as strong as he thought? Was this where it would all end? Or had his fate changed somehow?

For the first time since he had embarked, Thor took seriously the idea that he might not return. For some reason, he thought of Gwendolyn. He thought of her waiting for him, of his never showing up, of his not returning for her. It broke his heart.

Before he could finish the thought, suddenly, from out of the cave came the largest beast Thor had ever seen. The Cyclops took three huge steps, ducking his head, unbelievably, despite the thirty foot opening, then raising himself to his full height as he stepped outside. He was enormous, like looking up at a mountain.

As he stepped, the earth shook. He leaned back and roared, and it felt as if it would shatter Thor's eardrums. Thor's body froze with fright. Finally, Malic's did, too. He stood there, open-mouthed, staring up, his sword hanging limp in his hand. Krohn snarled, fearless.

The Cyclops must have been fifty feet tall. He was broader and thicker than an elephant, the grey skin on his muscles rippling, his one eye blinking madly, and had two huge fangs, each the size of Thor. He leaned his head back and roared again, his hands bunched into fists, his arms rising high then coming down, too fast, like tree trunks, swinging right for Thor and Malic.

Thor jumped out of the way just in time, as the monster's fists slammed into the earth, creating a huge crater, shaking the ground so hard that Thor stumbled. Malic barely escaped, too.

Thor looked at the short sword in his hand, at the sling at his waist, and wondered how he could ever combat this creature. He was a speck next to this beast; Thor doubted his sword could even puncture its skin. It would take an army, and an arsenal of weapons, to even attempt to kill it.

Malic threw caution to the wind. He raised his sword, and with a battle cry, charged the creature, attempting to puncture the beast in its shin. But he did not even get close: the beast merely swatted him away, and Malic went flying, landing hard on the ground, rolling and tumbling.

The beast turned to Thor. It charged him, the ground shaking as it went, and Thor was too frozen with fear to move. Thor wanted to turn and run, but he forced himself to stand in place, to hold his ground. There were too many eyes watching him; he could not let down his Legion brothers. He remembered what one of his trainers taught him: it was okay to feel fear—but it was not okay to give into it. That was the code of a warrior.

So instead, Thor forced himself to be strong. He forced himself to draw his sword, to step forward, and swing for the monster's calf. It was a direct hit.

But the monster's skin was so thick, the sword merely bounced off, falling from Thor's hands. It was like striking stone. Thor scurried to pick it up again. The creature, angered, swung its huge fist at Thor; Thor managed to duck, and he saw his chance. He darted forward, raised his sword high, and plunged it in the beast's smallest toe.

The beast shrieked as rivers of blood poured out. It was an awful noise, shaking Thor to the very core—so horrific, Thor almost wished he had never attacked it.

The beast was much faster than Thor anticipated. Before Thor could react, he swept down again with one hand, and this time grabbed Thor and hoisted him high into the air. He squeezed Thor so hard, he could barely breathe.

The beast raised Thor higher up, all the way.

Krohn, down below, snarled and charged the Cyclops. He sank his teeth into its toe, and dug in, shaking it, until finally the Cyclops, infuriated, threw Thor down.

Thor felt himself go flying through the air and land hard on the ground, rolling several times, covered in dust, winded.

The beast roared again, then reached down and swiped for Krohn, who got out of the way just in time. It then yanked Thor's short sword out from his toe as if it were a toothpick, and snapped the sword in half with a single hand.

The beast stepped towards him, and as Thor lay there, watching, helpless, he was sure he was dead.

But then the beast surprised him. It stopped, turned and looked at Malic instead. In one quick motion, it swooped down, grabbed Malic, and lifted him high into the air, squeezing him harder than he had Thor. Malic shrieked, and Thor could hear his ribs breaking even from here.

The beast held Malic close, right to his face, as if relishing this. Malic squirmed in his arms, but it was useless.

The beast suddenly pulled Malic to him, opened his mouth, revealing rows of jagged teeth, then brought Malic face first into his mouth. He chomped down, biting off Malic's head. Blood came gushing down like a river. It happened so fast, Thor could barely process what he had witnessed.

The Cyclops dropped to the ground what was left of Malic's body.

It then stopped and turned to Thor, staring at him, and Thor's heart slammed in his chest. He prayed that the legend was true, that the monster would only kill the guilty.

Finally, after what felt like an eternity, the beast slowly turned its back, and marched to its cave. Thor held his breath, beginning to realize that the nightmare was over.

Thor could not believe it. His trial had taken place, in the eyes of his brethren, and he had been vindicated. He would live.

CHAPTER SEVENTEEN

Gareth walked slowly into the throne room, needing time to be alone, to gather his thoughts, to remember why he wanted to be King. He entered the immense chamber, with its vaulted ceilings, stone floor and walls, and crossed it slowly, head down, his mind racing as he walked in the path his father had so many times.

Halfway across the room, Gareth looked up—and froze in place.

To his surprise, his throne had been turned around in the middle of the night, so its back was to him. Even more surprising, there was somebody sitting in it. In *his* throne.

Gareth could see the outline of a body, the arms resting on its arms, and he burned with rage, wondering who could be so impudent as to sit on a king's throne. He also was puzzled as to how they had managed to turn around the throne, this ancient seat that had been rooted to its place for a thousand years.

Gareth walked quickly towards it, prepared to confront the intruder.

As he reached the base of the steps, to his shock, the throne suddenly spun around. On it, facing him, looking down, sat his father, his eyes open in disapproval.

Gareth stood unmoving, breathless, feeling as if a sword had been thrust into his chest. His feet were stuck to the floor: he could not get himself to pick them up, to put one after the other to ascend the stairs. After all, it was his father's throne. And now his father was seated in it. He did not know how it was possible.

"The weight of my blood hangs on you," his father proclaimed. "It is a weight you will not escape. Blood will have blood."

Gareth blinked—and when he opened his eyes, the throne sat empty. He breathed hard, looking all around, wondering what had happened. He felt a presence lingering in the air, but his father was nowhere to be seen.

Legs shaking, Gareth ascended the ivory steps, one at a time, tentative, until finally he reached the throne. He sat in it, slowly, afraid to lean back. Gradually, he did, and looked out over the empty room.

Suddenly, he felt a horrific pain in his hands, his forearms, his thighs, even the back of his head. He looked down and saw the throne was now covered in thorns, growing thicker by the moment, rising up like an unstoppable vine, wrapping themselves around him, chaining him to it. The thorns grew wildly, embracing him, squeezing him, until he was bleeding all over his body. He struggled, leaned back and shrieked from the pain—until finally the thorns rose up and wrapped themselves around his mouth.

Gareth woke screaming.

He jumped from his bed in the muted light of dawn and paced his room, breathing hard. He made his way to the far wall, leaned a palm against the stone, and bent over, gasping for air.

It had felt so real, all of it. He spun around his room, almost expecting his father to be in it.

But he was not. He was alone.

Gareth felt haunted. He had an awful, sinking feeling that his father's spirit would not let him rest. Would never let him rest.

He needed answers. He needed to know his future, needed to know how all of this would end.

He paced, wracking his brain, when a figure popped into his mind: the witch.

Of course, she would know.

Gareth raced across the room, stopping only to put on his crown, his mantle, to carry his scepter, without which he would go nowhere. He needed answers—and fast.

*

Gareth marched quickly through the forest trail, heading deeper and deeper into Dark Wood, trying to shake the dark thoughts that had gripped him, that seemed to hang over him like a veil. His mind had not stopped racing since his dream, and he had found no respite in any corner of the castle. Everywhere he looked, he saw another monument to his father, felt another silent rebuke to his failure as a son, and now, his failure as King. He felt increasingly that this castle was a big tomb, a monument of ghosts, and that one day it would entomb him, too.

Blood will have blood.

His father's voice rang in his ears as he found himself reliving the dream, again and again.

As he pondered it all, pondered his failed hoisting of the Dynasty Sword, Gareth was struck with the idea that perhaps, after all, he was not destined to be King. Perhaps he was *never* destined to be king.

He needed prophecy, like a man in the desert needed water. The witch had seen his future when he had first visited her; he felt that she would have the answers he needed, would tell him honestly what his destiny was. Until he knew, he could not rest.

Gareth marched along the forest trail, heading deeper and deeper, ignoring the sky as it turned black, as thick clouds rolled in, and as a summer rain suddenly hailed down, lashing him. He twisted and turned through the trails of Dark Wood, trying to remember his way back. He had hoped it would be a place that he would never return to, and was unpleasantly surprised to find himself back here so quickly.

The air got colder and he sensed an evil energy getting closer. There was no doubt that this was the place. He could feel it hanging in the air, oozing onto his skin, like a slime, even from here.

As Gareth pushed deeper, hurrying between a clump of thick trees, he saw it: there, in the clearing, sat her small stone cottage. Even the trees around the clearing were recognizable: twisted into unnatural shapes, with three red trees on its edge, one in each direction.

Gareth strode across it, hurrying to her cottage, and as he reached her door, he lifted the brass knocker and slammed it several times. It echoed with a hollow thud, and he waited and waited, to no avail, getting drenched in the rain. The sky was now nearly as black as night, even though it was morning.

Gareth slammed the knocker again and again.

"OPEN THIS DOOR!" he screamed.

He was flooded with panic, wondering what he would do if she were gone from this place.

He waited what felt like an eternity, and was just about to turn away, when suddenly, the door opened.

Gareth spun and looked inside.

He could see no one, nothing but blackness, the faint flicker of a candle coming from deep inside. He turned, surveyed the woods, made sure no one was watching, then he hurried inside, slamming the door behind them.

It was quiet in here, the only sound that of the rain hitting the stone roof, of the rain dripping off of him, onto the floor in a small puddle. He looked around, giving his eyes time to adjust. It was so dim in here, he could barely see the witch, on the far side of the room, could barely see her silhouette. Hunched over, fiddling with something, she looked more creepy and ominous than before. The room was filled with her stench—that of decay and rotting flesh. He could hardly breathe. He already regretted coming here. Had it been a mistake?

"So," said the witch in her horse, mocking voice, "our new King comes to visit!"

She cackled, thrilled with her own statement. Gareth could not understand what was so funny. He hated her laughter. He hated everything about her.

"I have come for answers," he said, taking a step towards her, trying to sound confident, trying to sound like a king, but hearing the shakiness in his own voice.

"I know why you have come, *boy*," she spat. "For assurance that you will rule forever. That you will not be killed, the way you killed others. We always want for ourselves what we deny others, don't we?"

There came a long silence, as she slowly made her way closer to him. Gareth did not know whether to run from her or rebuke her. She held a single candle up to her face, covered in warts and etched with lines.

"I cannot give you what you do not have," she said slowly, breaking into an evil smile, revealing small, rotted teeth.

Gareth felt a chill climb up his back.

"What do you mean, 'do not have'?" he asked.

"Destiny is what it is, boy," she said.

"What does that mean?" he pressed urgently, having a sinking feeling. "Are you saying I'm not destined to be King?"

"There are many kings in this world. There are those greater than kings, too. Those with greater destinies—destinies that outshine yours."

"Greater than mine?" he asked. "But I am King of the Western Kingdom of the Ring! The greatest free land left in the Empire. Who could possibly be greater than me?"

"Thorgrin," she answered directly.

The name struck him like a knife.

"Thorgrin will be greater than you. Greater than all the MacGil Kings. Greater than any King that ever lived. And one day, you will bow down to him and beg him for mercy," she said, her voice cackling.

Gareth felt sick at her pronouncement—most of all, because it felt so real. He could hardly conceive how it could be. Thor? An outsider boy? A mere Legion member? Greater than he? With one wave of his hand he could have him imprisoned and executed. How could he possibly be greater than he?

"Then change my destiny!" he commanded, frantic. "Make ME the greatest! Make ME hoist the sword!"

The witch leaned back and cackled, until Gareth could stand it no longer.

"You would be crushed under the weight of that sword," she said. "You are king—for now. That should be enough. Make it enough. Because that is all you will ever have. And when what you have is done, you will pay the price. Blood will have blood."

He felt a chill.

"What good is it to be king, if the kingship will not last?" Gareth asked.

"What good is it to live, if death must come?" she answered.

"I am your king!" he yelled. "I COMMAND YOU! HELP ME!"

He charged for her, aiming to grab her by the shoulders, to shake her into submission—but as he reached for her, he felt himself grabbing at nothing but air.

He spun around, searched the cottage—but it was empty.

Gareth turned and stumbled from the cottage, into the sky, and as he got drenched, icy water running down his face and neck, he welcomed the pouring rain. He wished it would wash away his dreams, this meeting, and everything ill he had ever done. He no longer wanted to be king. He just wanted another chance at life.

"FATHER!" he shrieked.

His voice rose up, higher into Dark Wood, louder even than the sound of the rain—and was met by the cry of a distant bird.

*

Godfrey walked quickly down the forest trail as the sky darkened and a cool wind picked up, forking onto the trail that led to Dark Wood. The wind howled and the sky grew darker as he went, and he felt the hairs rise on the back of his neck. He could sense evil in this place. As the skies opened and rain came pouring down, now, more than ever, he wished he had a drink. Or two.

As the reality of what he was doing began to sink in, a part of him became afraid. After all, what if he found this witch, and what if he found answers he did not like. What could he really do? Was this witch dangerous? And if Gareth caught him asking, couldn't he have him imprisoned, too, along with Kendrick?

Godfrey doubled his pace, and as he rounded a small bend, he raised his head and was shocked at the sight. He stopped in his tracks, frozen. He could not believe it. Walking towards him, head down, mumbling to himself, was none other than his brother: Gareth.

143

Dressed in their father's finest robes, still wearing his father's crown and carrying his scepter, Gareth marched towards him, alone, emerging from Dark Wood. What was he doing here?

A moment later Gareth looked up and let out a little cry, just feet away, startled to see anyone there in the wood—let alone his brother.

"Godfrey!" Gareth exclaimed. "What are you doing here?"

"I should ask the same of you," Godfrey responded darkly.

Gareth scowled and Godfrey could sense their old sibling rivalry rekindled.

"You ask nothing of me," Gareth hissed. "You are my younger brother. And I am your King now, unless you have forgotten," he said in his sternest voice.

Godfrey let out a short, derisive laugh, raspy from years of drink and tobacco.

"You are king of nothing," Godfrey shot back. "You are just a pig. The same person you always were. You can fool the others, but not me. I never deferred to father's command—do you really think I would defer to yours?"

Gareth reddened, turning a shade of purple, but Godfrey could see that he'd caught him. Gareth knew his own brother, and knew that Godfrey would never bow down to him.

"You didn't answer my question," Gareth said. "What brings you here?"

Godfrey smiled, seeing how nervous Gareth was, and realizing he had him.

"Well, funny you should ask," Godfrey answered. "I remembered my walk the other day, bumping into you, and your evil sidekick, Firth. At the time, I thought nothing of it, of what you'd be doing out here, in Dark Wood. I must have assumed the two of you were taking a lover's walk."

Godfrey took a deep breath.

"But as I thought back on our father's murder, I remembered that day. And as I thought of the vial of poison used in the attempt to kill him, it occurred to me that maybe you came all the way out here for something more. Maybe it was not just an innocent stroll. Maybe you came here for something more ominous. Something potent enough to kill our father. Maybe a witch's brew. Maybe the same poison supposedly found in our brother Kendrick's chamber," Godfrey said, proud of himself for piecing it all together, and feeling more sure of it now than ever.

Godfrey watched Gareth's eyes closely as he pronounced each word, and he could see them shifting, could see how well Gareth tried to hide his reaction; but in those eyes, he could see that he had caught him. Everything he had said was true.

"You are a paranoid, wasteful drunk," Gareth scolded. "You always have been. You have no purpose for your life, so you imagine fancies for others. I can see that you try to make yourself important with these fanciful plots, try to be the hero of our dead father—but you are not. You are as low as the masses. In fact, you are even lower, because you had the potential to be more. Father hated you, and no one in this kingdom takes you seriously. How dare you try to implicate me in our father's murder? The rightful assassin is sitting in the dungeon, and the entire kingdom knows it. And babbling words from a drunk will change no one's mind."

Godfrey could hear, from the over-eagerness of Gareth's tone, that he was nervous. That he knew he was caught.

Godfrey smiled back.

"It's funny what a kingdom can believe from a drunk," he said, "when one speaks the truth."

Gareth scowled back.

"If you slander your King," Gareth threatened, "you better be prepared to prove it. If not, I shall have you executed with Kendrick."

"And who else shall you imprison?" Godfrey asked. "How many souls can you quash until our kingdom realizes that I am right?"

Gareth reddened, then suddenly brushed past Godfrey, bumping his shoulder roughly, and hurrying off down the trail.

Godfrey turned and watched him go, until he disappeared in the dark forest. He was convinced now. And more determined than ever.

He turned and looked down the trail leading towards a clearing in the distance. He knew that's where the witch's cottage was. He was just feet away from finding the proof he needed.

Godfrey turned and hurried down the trail, nearly running, stumbling over roots, going as fast as he could as the sky turned dark, the wind howling.

Finally, he burst through the trees, and entered the clearing. He sprinted into it, prepared to knock down the witch's door, to confront her, to get the proof he needed.

But as he entered the clearing, he stood there, frozen in his tracks. He didn't understand. He had been to this clearing before, had seen her cottage. But as he stood there now, the clearing was completely empty. There was no cottage, no building—nothing but grass. It was empty, surrounded by gnarled trees, three red trees. Had it disappeared?

The sky flashed and lightning struck the clearing, and Godfrey stood there and watched, baffled, wondering what dark forces were at play, what evil was sheltering his brother.

CHAPTER EIGHTEEN

Gwendolyn stood before her mother's chamber, her arm raised before the large, oak door, hesitating as she grabbed the iron knocker. She remembered the last time she had seen her mother, how badly it had went, the threats from both sides. She recalled her mother's forbidding her to see Thor again and her vowing to never see her again. They had both wanted what they wanted, at whatever cost. That was how it had always been between them. Gwen had always been her daddy's girl, and that had provoked her mother's wrath and jealousy.

Gwen was sure when she walked out on her that day that she would never see her again. Gwen considered herself a tolerant, forgiving person, but she also had her pride. She was like her father that way. And once someone wounded her pride, she would never talk to them again, under any circumstance.

And yet here she was, holding the cold, iron knocker, preparing to slam it, to ask her mother permission to speak with her and to plead for her help in freeing Kendrick from prison. It shamed her to find herself in this position, having to humble herself to approach her mother, to speak to her again—and no less, doing so in the context of needing her help. It was like conceding to her mother that she had won. Gwen felt torn to bits, and wished that she were anywhere but here. If it weren't for Kendrick, she would never give her the time of day again.

No matter what her mother said, Gwen would never change her mind when it came to Thor. And she knew her mother would never let that go.

But then again, since the death of her father, her mother had truly been a different person. Something had happened within her. Perhaps it had been a stroke—or perhaps it was something psychological. She hadn't spoken a word to anyone since that fateful day, had been in a nearly catatonic state, and Gwen didn't know what to expect. Perhaps her mother would not even be able to speak with her. Perhaps this was all a waste of time.

Gwen knew she should pity her—but despite herself, she was unable to. Her mother's new condition had been convenient for her—she was finally out of her hair, finally did not need to live in fear of all her vindictiveness. Before this happened, Gwen felt certain that she would begin to feel pressure from all sides to never see Thor again, to find herself married off to some cretin. She wondered if her father's death had truly changed her. Maybe it had humbled her, too.

Gwen took a deep breath and raised the knocker and slammed it, trying to think only of Kendrick, her brother who she loved so much, wallowing away in the dungeon.

She slammed the iron knocker again and again, and it resounded loudly in the empty corridors. She waited what felt like forever, until finally a servant opened the door and stared back cautiously. It was Hafold, the old nurse who had been her mother's attendant as long as she could remember. She was older than the Ring itself, and she stared back at Gwen disapprovingly. She was more loyal to her mother than anyone she knew; they were like the same person.

"What do you want?" she asked, curt.

"I'm here to see my mother," Gwen responded.

Hafold stared back disapprovingly.

"And why would you want to do that? You know your mother does not wish to see you. I presume you made it quite clear that you do not wish to see her, either."

Gwen stared back at Hafold, and it was her turn to give a disapproving stare. Gwen was feeling a new strength overcoming, her father's strength rising through her, and she felt less of a tolerance for all of these overbearing, authoritative types who wielded their disapproval on the younger generation like a weapon. What gave them all the right to be so superior, so disapproving of everyone and everything?

"It is not your place to question me, and it is not my place to have to explain myself to you," Gwen said back firmly. "You are a servant to this royal family. I am royalty, lest you forget. Now move out of my way. I am here to see my mother. I am not asking you—I am telling you."

Hafold's face fell in surprise; she stood there, wavering, then stepped out of the way as Gwen stormed past her.

Gwen took several steps into the room and as she did, she spotted her mother, seated at the far end of the chamber. She could see the broken chess pieces, still lying on the floor, the table on its side. Gwen was surprised to see her mother had left it that way. Then she realized that her mother probably wanted it as a reminder. Maybe it was a reminder to punish her. Or maybe their argument had gotten to her, after all.

Gwen saw her mother seated there, in her delicate yellow velvet chair, beside the window, facing out, the sunlight hitting her face. She wore no makeup, she was still dressed in yesterday's clothes, and her hair looked as if it had not been done in days. Her face looked old, sagging, lines etched where Gwen had not noticed them before. Gwen could hardly believe how much she had aged since her father's death—she barely recognized her. She could feel what a toll her father's death had taken on her, and despite herself, she felt some compassion for her. At least they had shared one thing in common: a love for her father.

"Your mother is not well," came Hafold's harsh voice, walking up beside her. "It will not do for you to disturb her now, whatever matter it is that you've come to inquire—"

Gwen spun.

"Leave us," Gwen commanded.

Hafold stared back, horrified.

"I will not leave your mother unattended. It is my duty to—"

"I said leave us!" Gwen screamed, pointing at the door. Gwen felt stronger, harsher than she ever had, and she could actually hear the authority of her father's voice coming through.

151

Hafold must have recognized it, too, must have recognized that this was no longer the young girl she had been accustomed to knowing. Her eyes open wide in surprise, and maybe fear, and she scowled, turned, and hurried from the room, slamming the door behind her.

Gwen crossed the room and locked the door; she did not want any more spies in here to hear what she was about to say.

She turned and went back to her mother's side. To Gwen's upset, her mother had not flinched, had not reacted to any of it; she remained seated there, staring out the window. She wondered if she could even speak anymore, if this was just a waste of time.

Gwen knelt by her side, reached up and placed a hand on hers, gently.

"Mother?" she asked, using her gentlest voice.

To Gwen's disappointment, there came no response. She felt her heart shattering. She did not know why, but she felt a tremendous sadness overcoming her. And somehow, for the first time, she felt herself able to understand her mother—and even to forgive her.

"I love you, mother," she said. "I'm sorry for all that has happened. I really am."

Despite herself, Gwen felt tears well up. She did not know if she was crying for the loss of her father, or for the lost chance of a relationship between her and her mother, or for all the pent-up grief she had felt since she and had her mother had fought. Whatever it was, it all came out now, and Gwen cried and cried.

After what felt like forever, nothing but her crying to fill the silence of the vast, empty chamber, to Gwen's surprise, her mother turned and looked at her. Her face was expressionless, her icy blue eyes wide open, but Gwen saw a quiver of something, thought she could see some part of her coming back to life.

"Your father is dead," her mother said.

The words came out like a grim proclamation, and even though she knew they were true, they were painful for Gwen to hear.

Gwen nodded slowly back.

"Yes he is," she responded.

"And nothing can bring him back," her mother added.

"Nothing," Gwen agreed.

Her mother turned back to the window. She sighed.

"I never thought it would end like this," she said.

And then she fell silent again, staring out at a distant cloud passing by.

After it went on for too long, after Gwen feared she might be losing her again, Gwen reached up and squeezed her wrist.

"Mother," she urged, wiping away tears with the back of her hand. "I need your help. Your son, Kendrick, lies wallowing in the dungeon. He was put there by your other son, Gareth. He's been accused of father's murder. You know that Kendrick would not commit this murder. Kendrick is set to be executed. You must not let this happen."

Gwen knelt there, squeezing her mother's hand, waiting urgently for a response.

She waited what felt like forever. She was about to give up hope, when suddenly her mother's eyes flickered.

"Kendrick is not my son," she said, matter-of-factly, still watching the sky. "He is your father's boy. Of another woman."

"That is true," Gwen said, nervous. "But you raised him as your own. Your husband loved him as a son. You know that. And, whether he was true or not, Kendrick always viewed you as a mother. He has no one else. As you said, our father is dead. It is left to you to defend him. If you do nothing, if you do not act, on the morrow, he will be dead—for a murder he did not commit. The murder of your husband. His execution would stain your husband's memory."

Gwen felt proud of herself for laying it all out, and she felt that her mother heard every word of it. There followed a long silence.

"I do not rule this land," her mother said. "I am just another former Queen. Powerless, as the rest. The men rule in this kingdom."

"You are *not* powerless," Gwen insisted. "You are the mother of the current King. You are a former queen to the former King, who died but days ago—and who are country still loves and mourns. All of his counselors and advisers still listen to you. They trust you. They love you, if for no other reason than they loved him. A command from you would hold much weight. It would prevent Kendrick's death."

154

Her mother sat there, staring out, her expression barely changing. Gwen watched her eyes, but could not tell how much she was truly processing, how much she was capable of taking in. She seemed as sharp as ever, but clearly, something had happened within her.

"Wouldn't you like to find your husband's murderer?" Gwen asked.

Her mother shrugged.

"It is not for me to intervene in my son's rule. He is King now. The fates must play out as they must."

"So will you just sit there, then, and do nothing as your innocent son dies?"

Slowly, the former queen shook her head.

"Gareth was always a willful boy. My firstborn son," the queen said. "I believe that he carried all of my sins. His nature could never be corrected. Perhaps he killed your father. Perhaps not. But kings are meant to be killed. They're meant to be deposed. Your father knew that. It is the risk one takes when assuming the throne.

"Of course I mourn for my husband," she added. "But that is the dance of crowns."

Gwen fumed. She stared at her mother, saw her resolve, and felt a newfound hatred for her.

Gwen stood and scowled down at her, preparing this time to never see her again. She took one long last look at her, to ingrain her face in her memory. It was a face she never wanted to forget—a face she never wanted to become.

"Our father looks down at you in disgrace," Gwen said, feeling as if she were channeling her father's voice.

With that, she turned, crossed the room, opened the door and slammed it behind her, its echo shaking the entire castle.

CHAPTER NINETEEN

Thor sat with the other Legion members, and Krohn, on the ground in their makeshift camp at the top of the cliff, their roaring fire doing little to fend off the black of night. Dozens of them sat spaced around it, all exhausted, staring somberly into the flames. Thor looked back and saw the sky, alight with thousands of stars, reds and yellows and greens, positioned in such a way that Thor had never seen before in this part of the world. The fire cracked, but other than that, the night was silent.

They had all been sitting there for hours, frozen with exhaustion, pondering their fates after this grueling day of training. Thor, especially, was stung by his encounter with the Cyclops. He felt vindicated in the eyes of his brothers in arms, who looked at him now with a new respect. But he also felt shaken. He thought of how close he had come to dying, and wondered for the millionth time about the mystery of life. Just yesterday, Malic had been sitting with them all; now, he was dead. Where had he gone? Who might go next?

Kolk cleared his throat, and the boys turned and looked at him. He sat there, in the circle along with the others, resting his forearms on his knees, back erect, frowning into the fire. His eyes were wide open, and it looked as if he were remembering something vividly. The boys had been promised a tale around the fire, one of conquest and past glories. But they had been waiting for hours, and none came. Thor had assumed it was not going to come. But now, as Kolk cleared his throat, Thor settled in and prepared to listen. Beside him, Reese, O'Connor, Elden and the twins did the same.

"Twenty sun cycles ago," Kolk began, staring into the flames, his voice somber, "before most of you were born, when I was the age of the eldest of you, when King MacGil was still alive, when he was just a prince and we fought side-by-side, there came the battle which gave me this scar," he said, turning his cheek to reveal the long, jagged scar which ran along his jawbone.

"That day started out as any other. MacGil, Brom and I, with a dozen other legion members, were on patrol. Deep in the valley of the Nevaruns. The Nevaruns are separatists: they live on the far reaches of the southern provinces of the Ring. They are rebels—they owe allegiance to the MacGils, but are always threatening to align with one lord or other and break off from the kingdom. They are also tough, cruel people, who do not defer to authority. They have been a thorn in the MacGil's side for centuries. They are half-breeds, part human and part something else. They have eight fingers and toes, and are twice as broad as the average man. It is said that humans mated with something else to breed them, centuries ago. Nobody knows what.

"The Nevaruns are a fierce people," Kolk continued. "They don't respect our code of ethics, of laws of chivalry. They fight to win—at any cost."

Kolk breathed deep, eyes closed, remembering.

"It was a cold and windy day. Walking through a narrow valley, after days of silent patrol, we were ambushed. Several of them jumped us from behind, knocking me off my horse. One of them knocked me down with a spear, while another came up from behind, stabbed me in the back and then used his knife to do this handiwork," he said, pointing at his jaw.

Thor swallowed at the thought of it, of what Kolk must have gone through. Even now, twenty sun cycles later, as he stared into the flames, it seemed as if Kolk were reliving it.

"I would have died if it were not for MacGil, who, luckily, had to relieve himself, and was catching up. He was fifty paces behind me, and they didn't see him. He sent an arrow through their backs."

Kolk sighed.

"I was foolish, and that is the point of this tale. I expected the enemy to fight on my terms. To meet me in the open. To challenge and face me as a man, as any warrior should. Not to be cowardly and jump me from behind, not to fight with two men against one, not to wait until I was in a space so narrow I could not maneuver. And this is what you must remember: your enemy will *never* fight on your terms. He will fight on *his*. War for you means something else to him. What you consider fair and noble, he does not. You must be prepared, at all times, for anything.

"That does not mean you sink to his level. You must fight at all times with our code of honor and chivalry—or else you will lose the spirit of the

159

warrior, which is what sustains you. The day you begin to fight as them is the day you lose your soul. Better to die with honor than to win in disgrace."

With that, Kolk fell silent, and a deep silence enveloped all the boys around him. For a long while the only sound was that of the whipping of the wind high up on the cliff, of the distant crash of the ocean, somewhere on the horizon.

And then, some time later, came the sound of a distant roar, like thunder. Thor turned, as did the others, and saw something light up the horizon. He stood, with Reese and a few others, to go look.

Thor walked over to the cliff's edge and looked out at the black night, the horizon lit by a world of stars, their light strong enough to illuminate the swirling red waters of the ocean beneath them. In the distance, far off, Thor could see a red glow. It came in short bursts, then stopped, like a volcano shooting up lava that lit up the night, then just as quickly faded out. There followed another rumbling sound.

"The cry of the Dragon," came a voice.

Thor looked over, and standing there, set apart from the others, his back to him, staring out over the cliff and holding his staff, was Argon. Thor was shocked to see him.

Thor turned away from the other boys, and walked over to him. He stood beside him and waited until he was ready, knowing better than to disturb him.

"How did you get here?" Thor asked, amazed. "What are you doing here?"

Argon stood there, expressionless, ignoring Thor, still staring out at the horizon.

Thor finally turned and looked at the horizon with him, standing by his side, waiting, trying to be patient, to accept conversation on Argon's terms.

"The Dragon's breath," Argon observed. "This is a dragon that chooses to live apart. You are in his land. He is not pleased."

Thor thought about that.

"But we are to be here for a hundred days," Thor said, worried.

Argon turned and looked at him.

"If he chooses to let you," he responded. "These shores are littered far and wide with the bones of warriors who thought they could conquer the dragon. The pride of man is the feast of dragons."

Thor swallowed, beginning to realize how precarious the Hundred was.

"Will I survive it?" he asked, hoping for a response.

"Your time to die has not yet come," Argon responded slowly.

Thor felt immensely relieved to hear that, and surprised that Argon would give him a straight answer. He decided to push his luck.

"Will I also become a member of the Legion?" he asked.

"That, and much more," Argon replied.

Thor's spirits lifted even higher. He could not believe he was getting answers out of Argon. He felt a sudden burning curiosity to know why Argon was here. He knew he would not have come here, would not be talking to him, unless he had something important to say.

"Do you see the horizon?" Argon asked. "Beyond the Dragon's breath? Past the flames? Out there, in the blackness, lies your destiny."

Thor sensed what he was speaking of. He remembered MacGil's dying words, about his destiny, about his mother.

"My mother?" Thor asked.

Slowly, Argon nodded.

"She is alive? She is out there? In the Land of the Druids? Is that it?"

Argon turned to him, his eyes aglow.

"Yes," he answered. "She awaits you even now. You have a great destiny to fulfill."

Thor was excited beyond belief at the idea of his mother being alive somewhere in the world, at the idea of meeting her, discovering who she was. He was excited at the idea that someone was awaiting him, that someone cared for him. But he was also confused.

"But I thought my destiny was back home, in the Ring?" Thor asked.

Argon shook his head.

"A greater part awaits you out there. Greater than you can ever imagine. The fate of the Ring rests on it. There is great unrest at home. The Ring needs you."

Thor could scarcely comprehend it. How could the Ring need him, just a single boy?

"Tell me, Thor, what do you see? Look into the blackness. Close your eyes. What do you see in the Sorcerer's Ring?"

Thor did as instructed, closing his eyes, breathing deeply. He tried to focus, to allow whatever it was to come to him.

But whatever power he had, he could not summon it. He could not focus.

"Be patient," came Argon's voice. "Don't force it. Allow it to come to you. You can see it. I know you can."

Thor kept his eyes closed, breathed, again and again, and tried to let go of controlling it.

Then, he was shocked. He began to see something. Great visions, lucid, as if he were witnessing them. He saw destruction in the Ring. Murders. Fires. Rubble. He was horrified.

"I see great calamity," he said, struggling to comprehend his visions. "I see death. Battle. Destruction. I see the kingdom collapsing."

"Good," Argon said. "Yes, tell me more."

Thor furrowed his brow.

"I see a great darkness in Gareth."

"Yes," Argon said.

Thor opened his eyes and looked at Argon, distraught.

"Gwendolyn," he said. "What about her? I can't it clearly. But I sense something. Something dark. Something I did not like. Tell me it's not true."

Argon turned away, looked into the blackness.

"We each have our own destiny, I'm afraid," he sighed.

"But I must save her!" Thor exclaimed. "From whatever it is, from whatever dark thing that is going to happen to her."

"You will save her," Argon said. "And you won't."

"What does that mean?" Thor pleaded. "Please, tell me. I beg you. No more riddles."

Argon slowly shook his head.

"You have come here to learn to be a warrior. Yet the physical is but one side of a warrior. You must learn to develop your inner skills. Your powers. Your ability to see. Don't get caught up in swords and spears. That is the easy route."

Argon turned and took a step closer to him, and stared into his eyes with burning intensity.

"The greatest battle ahead of you lies within yourself."

100 DAYS LATER

CHAPTER TWENTY

Gareth sat in his father's throne room, on his father's throne, looking down at the dozens of councilmen and lords and commoners before him, all with their own problems, and he was miserable. Months had passed since he had assumed the throne, and with each passing day, he felt more tortured, more paranoid—and more alone. He had ousted his closest friend and advisor—Firth—long ago, relegating him to the horse stables and forbidding him to see him, and he missed him. Ousting Firth was the right thing to do—he was reckless and had become a liability. After all, he remained the only one who could connect Gareth to his father's murder, and he did not want to be associated with him anymore.

He had brought in a half dozen of his friends to be his mentors, and it was these people who surrounded him these days. They were ruthless, ambitious, aristocratic types—and that was exactly what he wanted. Gareth didn't necessarily trust them, but at least they were his age, and they were as cynical and ruthless as he. They were the kind of people he wanted to surround himself with. They saw the world as he did, and he needed the new guard to counteract the old. His father's people were still entrenched, like an institution, and he felt increasingly oppressed by them. If he could, he would raze King's Court and build the whole thing anew. Everything new. He held no respect for history—he despised history. For him, the ideal was a modern, blank slate, and the destruction of every history book that ever was.

"My liege," said yet another commoner, as he stepped before him and bowed.

Gareth sighed, bracing himself for yet another petition. All day long, petty matters had been brought before him. He'd had no idea that ruling a kingdom could be so mundane; this was never how he had envisioned being King. One person after another streamed in, all wanting answers, judgments, and an endless stream of decisions needed to be made. Everyone wanted something, and everything seemed so trivial. Gareth had imagine being king more glorious.

Gareth looked to the stained glass window, high above his head, and he longed to be outside—to be anywhere but here. He was deeply bored. He felt something stirring inside him, and whenever he felt that way, he knew he had to break up the monotony of his life and create some trouble, some havoc for those around him.

"My lord," the commoner continued, "the land had been in my family for a thousand years."

Gareth sighed, trying to tune it all out. These stupid peasants had been going on about some land dispute for he did not know how long. He could barely follow it, and he'd had enough. He just wanted them out of his sight. He wanted time to be alone, to think about his father, about any details of the murder that could be discovered. About whether the witch would reveal him. He had felt profoundly uneasy since their confrontation, and was feeling increasingly paranoid that a conspiracy was tightening around him. He wondered incessantly over whether he would be found out. Ousting Firth had allayed his fears somewhat, but not entirely.

"My lord, that is not true," said another peasant. "That vineyard was planted by my father's ancestors. It encroached on his territory only through growth. But our territory, in turn, was encroached by his cattle."

Gareth looked down at them both, annoyed at being jolted from his thoughts. He did not know how his father had put up with all of this. He'd had enough.

"Neither of you shall have the land," Gareth said finally, annoyed. "I declare your land confiscated. It is now property of the King. You may both find new homes. That is all—now leave me."

The commoners stared back in stunned silence, mouths open in shock.

"My liege," said Aberthol, his ancient advisor, who sat seated with the other councilmembers at the semi-circular table. "Something like that has never been done in the history of the MacGils. This is not royal land, that much is certain. We cannot confiscate land from—"

"I said leave me!" Gareth yelled.

"But my Lord, if you take my land, where shall I and my family go?" asked the peasant. "We have lived on that land for generations!"

"You can be homeless," Gareth snapped, then motioned to his guards, who hurried forward and dragged the peasants from his sight.

"My liege! Wait!" one of them screamed.

But they were dragged from the room and the door slammed behind them.

The room hung with a heavy silence.

"Who else?" Gareth yelled, impatient to be done.

A group of nobles stood there, in the wings, and looked at each other hesitantly. Finally, they stepped forward.

There were six of them, barons from the northern province, aristocrats, dressed in the blue silk of their clan. Gareth recognized them instantly: the annoying lords who had burdened his father throughout his rule. They controlled the northern armies, and always held the royal family hostage, demanding as much from them as they could.

"My liege," said one of them, a tall, thin man in his fifties with a balding head, who Gareth remembered seeing from the time he was a boy, "we have two issues to put forth today. The first is the McClouds. Reports are spreading of raids into our villages. They have never raided this far north, and it is troubling. It may be prelude to a greater attack—a full scale invasion."

"Nonsense!" Orsefain exclaimed, one of Gareth's new advisors, who sat to his right. "The McClouds have never invaded, and they never would!"

"With all due respect," the lord countered, "you are too young to remember, but there have, in fact, been McCloud attempts at invasion, before your time. I remember them. It is possible, my lord. In any case, our people are alarmed. We request that you double your forces in our area, if for no other reason than to appease the people."

Gareth sat there, silent, impatient. He trusted his young advisor, and also doubted the McClouds would invade. He saw this request merely as a way for the northern nobles to try to manipulate him and his forces. It was time to let them know who ran the kingdom.

"Request denied," Gareth stated. "What else?"

The nobles looked at each other, unpleased. Another one of them cleared his throat and stepped forward.

"During your father's time, my liege, taxes were raised on our province to muster the northern armies in times of trouble. Your father had always promised to reduce taxes back to what they were, and before his death, the law was about to go into effect. But it was never ratified. So we ask to you to fulfill your father's will and lower the taxes on our people."

Gareth resented these barons, who thought they could dictate to him how to run his kingdom. Whether they liked it or not, he was still king. He had to show them who wielded the power here. He turned to Amrold, another new advisor.

"And what do you think, Amrold?" he asked.

Amrold sat there, narrowing his eyes at the lords, scowling down. He was a perpetually unhappy person, and that was one of the reasons Gareth loved him.

"You should not lower taxes," Amrold said, "but raise them. It's time for the north to understand who controls this Ring."

The nobles, along with Gareth's elder councilmembers, all gasped in outrage.

"My liege, who are these young folk you turn to for counsel?" Aberthol asked.

"These men you see behind me are part of my new council. They shall be included in all decisions we make," Gareth said.

"But my Liege, this is an outrage!" Kelvin said. "There have always been twelve councilmembers that advised the king, for centuries. It has never changed, not for any MacGil. It was the way your father had it, and the way we have always had it. You change the very nature of the kingship. We have been tested with years of wisdom. These new folk you bring in—they have no wisdom or experience!"

"It is my kingship to change as I will," Gareth shot back, firmly. He figured that now was the time to put all these old folk in their place. They were all biased towards his father anyway, and they had always hated him. He could see the resentment in their every glance.

"I shall fill my council with a hundred people if I like," Gareth added, "and turn to whomever I choose for advice. If you are unhappy, then leave now."

The old councilmen sat at their table, facing him, and he could see the look of surprise on their faces—which was exactly what he had wanted. He wanted these new advisors to keep them on edge. He was sending them a message: they were the old guard, that they were no longer needed.

Kelvin rose from the council table.

"I resign, my lord," he said.

"As do I," Duwayne echoed, standing with him.

They both turned their backs on him, and strode from the room.

Gareth watched them go, his face burning with indignation.

"Guards, arrest them!" Gareth yelled.

The guards stopped them at the door, shackled them, and led them away. Gareth could hear the muted screams of those councilmembers outside the room.

The other councilmembers stood.

"My Liege, this is an outrage! How can you arrest them? You just told them to leave!"

"I told them they were free to choose to leave," Gareth said. "But of course, that would be treason to the King. I will not abide traitors. Would any more of you like to leave?"

The councilmen looked at each other, distraught; they now had genuine doubt and fear in their eyes. They all looked like broken men—which was exactly what Gareth wanted. Inwardly, he smiled. He was dismantling his father's institutions, one person at a time.

"Be seated," Gareth ordered.

Slowly, reluctantly, the councilmembers sat back down.

Gareth turned to the nobles, who still stood there, awaiting his response. Now they needed to be put in their place.

"Regarding your taxes," Gareth said to them, "not only will I not lower them, but I shall raise them. As of today, your taxes are doubled. Do not come here again unless I summon you. That is all."

The lead baron's face quivered, then turned a shade of crimson. Gareth could see that this man was not used to being talked to in this way, and he enjoyed how upset he had made him.

"My liege, our people will not suffer this form of mistreatment."

Gareth stood, turning red himself.

"Yes, they *will* suffer it. Because I am King now. Not my father. And you answer to me. Now leave me. And don't show your face here again!"

The lords stared back at Gareth, mouths open in shock. Not a pin drop could be heard in the chamber, not among the dozens of attendants or councilmen or nobles seated and standing everywhere.

The group of nobles slowly turned, and marched out the chamber, their boots echoing. They slammed the door behind them.

As they went, Gareth noticed their conspiratorial glances. He could see in their eyes their resolve to overthrow him. He already could sense all the enemies in his court, all the plans to depose him. He would deal with each of them, one at a time. He would imprison every single one if he had to.

"Is that all then?" Gareth hastily asked the remaining councilmembers, slowly sitting back down.

"My liege," Aberthol said, tired, his voice broken, "all that remains is the investigation into your father's death."

"Of what do you speak?" Gareth demanded. "The investigation is closed. My brother Kendrick has been imprisoned."

"I'm afraid it is not so simple, my lord," Aberthol said. "The Silver is fiercely loyal to Kendrick. They are unsatisfied with his imprisonment. The staying of the execution helped, but not for long. There is great dissatisfaction among the ranks, especially after you cut their salary, and they call for a new investigation. You risk a revolt otherwise."

"But the vial of poison was found in Kendrick's chamber," Gareth protested, his heart pounding.

"Yet there remains no definitive proof linking Kendrick to the murder."

"As of today, I declare the investigation over," Gareth announced. "Kendrick will wallow in that dungeon every day of his life."

"But my lord—"

"Do not bring this matter up to me again," Gareth snapped. "Now leave me! All of you!"

Quickly, the room filed out, and Gareth found himself alone, sitting on the throne in the deep silence.

Gareth sat there, his heart pounding, seething; he had feared something like this might happen if Kendrick was not executed immediately. He fumed as he remembered, a few months ago, his mother's sudden interference, her using her powers to prevent him from executing Kendrick. He had heard that Gwen had gotten to her, that they had teamed up to stop it. He seethed with hatred for them both. He could not be safe as long as they were alive.

He recalled his bumbled attempt to have his man torture Gwen, months back. It hadn't worked. Perhaps now was time to try again. This time, he could outright kill her.

Gareth smiled, as a plan hardened in his mind. Yes, this time might just do the trick.

CHAPTER TWENTY ONE

Thor stood alone at the helm of a large, empty boat, in the middle of the ocean, the tides pulling him along at tremendous speed. The sails were bent by the wind, even though there was no one but him on the boat. It was a ghost ship, and he stood at its helm, looking out at the horizon, which was covered in an unearthly mist, golds and yellows and whites sparkling in the morning sun.

As the mist drifted, the outline of an island began to take shape, more of a mountain rising up from the sea than an island, its single peak soaring into the sky. It rose higher than any mountain Thor had ever seen, and at its top sat a castle, emerging from the rock, built into the edge of a cliff. The sky was expansive, filled with greens and pale yellows, a huge crescent moon hanging in its corner. The place was eerie and mystical. It seemed alive.

As Thor stood there, his boat rocking, somehow he was not afraid. He felt the ocean taking him there, and knew that this was the place he was meant to be. He knew, somehow, that his destiny awaited him there. That it was a place he was meant to be. That, in a strange way, it was home.

Thor could not remember setting sail, or how he got on this boat, but he knew it was a journey he was meant to take. Somehow, this place had always been in his dreams, somewhere deep down in the corners of his consciousness. He felt with certainty that his mother lived there.

Thor had never really contemplated his mother before. He had always been told she had passed away in childbirth, and had always felt a supreme guilt over this. But now, as he got closer to this island, he sensed her presence. That she was waiting for him.

A huge wave suddenly lifted the boat, hoisted it higher and higher into the air, and Thor felt himself rising higher and higher in the ocean. The wave picked up speed, like a tsunami, and he rode it all the way as it brought him rushing towards the island, faster and faster.

As he got close, he began to see a figure. It was a lone figure, standing atop a cliff. A woman. She wore flowing, blue robes, her chin was lowered, and her palms were out at her side. An intense light shone from behind her, radiated from her palms, shooting out like lightning. The light shone so brightly, that as Thor looked up, trying to see her, he had to shield his eyes. He could not make out her face.

He sensed that it was her. More than anything, he wanted to see her face, to see if she looked like him.

"Mother!" he called out.

"My son," came a soft voice from somewhere. It was the kindest, most reassuring voice he had ever heard. He longed to hear it again.

Suddenly, the wave came crashing down, and took the boat plunging down with it, and he braced himself as he headed for the rocks.

Thor woke with a start, sitting upright, breathing hard.

The dawn was breaking over the horizon, and all around him, the Legion members were strewn about, fast asleep. His mind spun with the dream: it had seemed so real.

As he got his bearings, he realized that today was the day. The final day of the Hundred. The day they had all been dreading.

He felt a hundred years older than when he'd arrived here a hundred days ago. He could not believe that he had made it, and that this was his final day. His time here had far exceeded his imagination. Each day been harder than the next, each training more grueling, pushing him and his brothers harder and harder. Days became longer and longer, as he had learned to train with every weapon known to man—and some not even known to man. They had been forced to train in every possible terrain, from swamps to glaciers, and had been screamed at from early morning to late at night. More than one of his brothers had dropped out, had been sent home alone on a small ship. Many had been injured. Two had died accidentally, slipping off a cliff on a particularly stormy day. They had all encountered trials and tribulations together, fought against monsters, survived every type of weather. This island was unforgiving, and had gone from hot to cold with no warning, seeming to have only two seasons.

As Thor sat there, Krohn beside him, a part of him dreaded this final day, wanted to lie back down, to go back to sleep—but he knew he could not. These last hundred days had forged him into a different person, and he was ready to face whatever they would throw at him.

Thor sat there in the early morning light, waiting. Soon, they would all arise, gear up, embark on their final mission. But until they did, he could revel in being the first to rise, and sit there and enjoy the silence, watch the sun break one final time over this place he had come to love.

*

Thor stood with the others on the rocky, narrow beach, hands on his hips, looking out at the storm tossed sea, feeling the chill in the air of the new season. He had learned to become so used to adverse weather that he no longer shivered as a freezing gale brushed across his body. He stared out at the sea, his grey eyes glistening, and felt hardened, impervious. He felt like a man.

His brothers in arms stood close by, Krohn beside him, near the fleet of small wooden boats preparing to set sail for the final test of the Hundred. They waited, all anxious, as Kolk paced among them, looking as dissatisfied and intense as ever.

"Those of you who have made it to this day might want to congratulate yourselves. Don't. You have one final day left, and this day is what sets others apart. If you survive it, you will come back a Legion member. All the trials you have been through, they have all just been preparation for what you're about to do."

Kolk stopped and turned, pointing at the horizon.

"That island on the horizon," he said, "on it lives a lone dragon, an outcast from the land of the dragons. We have lived in his shadow these past hundred days, and have been fortunate he has not attacked. Warriors do their best to avoid the place. Today, we will pay it a visit.

"This dragon jealously guards a treasure. An ancient, golden scepter. He is rumored to hide it deep in his lair. You must find the canyon, descend into it, find the scepter and return with it."

There came a nervous murmur from the group as the boys turned and looked at each other, fear filling their eyes. Thor's heart pounded as he looked out at the crashing sea, at the island in the distance, covered in a surreal mist, even on this clear day. He could feel its energy, even from here. Over the last hundred days his power had developed, and he was now able to be more sensitive to sensing energies, even from a distance. He could sense that a formidable creature lived on it, an ancient, primordial creature, and that they were heading into great danger.

"Man the boats and move!" Kolk commanded.

They all ran for the small rowboats, which were rocking wildly in the waters on shore, and one at a time they piled in, each boat holding about a dozen boys. Thor piled in, Krohn beside him, next to Reese, O'Connor, Elden and the twins, each sitting on a bench and grabbing an oar.

Before they pushed off, Thor looked to see William standing on shore, fear in his eyes. Thor had actually been surprised that William had made it this far, expecting him to drop out every step of the way. But now, this final exercise must have been too much for him.

"I said get in that boat!" Kolk yelled, hurrying up to him, the last boy left on the beach.

William stared back, wide-eyed.

"I'm sorry, sir, but I can't do it," he said meekly.

Thor sat there, his boat rocking wildly, and his heart dropped for William. He did not want to see him go—not after all they'd been through.

"I'm not going to tell you again," Kolk warned. "You don't get in that boat now, you're out of the Legion. Everything you've done will be for nothing. Forever."

William stood there and shook his head.

"I'm sorry," William said. "I wish I could. This is one thing I cannot do."

"I can't do it either," came a voice.

Thor looked over, and saw another boy, one of the older ones, jump out of one of the other boats, and stand on shore. They both stood there on the sand, their heads down in shame.

Kolk sneered, grabbed each from behind and shoved them forward, away from the other boys. Thor felt terrible for them. He knew they would be put on the small boat and sent back to the Ring, and carry that stigmatism with them for the rest of their lives.

Before Thor could think of it too deeply, the Legion's commanders came up behind each boat, and gave each a strong shove, pushing it into the sea. Thor felt his boat moving under him, and moments later he was taking up his oar, with the others.

The churning of the sea grew stronger as they went, and soon they were far from shore, stuck in strong tides, pulling them towards the dragon's isle.

As they neared it, Thor tried to get a better view, but it was constantly obscured by the mist clinging to its shores.

"I hear the dragon that lives there eats a man a day for breakfast," O'Connor said.

"Of course they would save something like this for the final day," Elden said. "Just when we thought we were getting out of here."

Reese looked at the horizon.

"I've heard stories of this place from my brothers," he said. "The power of the dragon is unfathomable. There is no way we could all defeat it head-on, even together. We just have to hope we tread carefully and don't rouse him. The island is big enough, and he may be sleeping. All we have to do is survive the day."

"And what are the chances of that?" O'Connor asked.

Reese shrugged.

"I heard that not all boys survived in years past," he said. "But enough did."

Thor's anxiety increased as the tides picked up, pulling them towards the island. The rowing got easier, and soon he could make out the distinct outline of its shores, comprised of red rocks of infinite shape and size, shining, glowing, as if they were on fire. They sparkled in the light, like a beach of rubies. He had never seen anything like it.

"Orethist," Conval said, looking at the rocks. "Legend has it that if you give one to someone you love, it will save their life."

Moments later their boat landed on shore, and Thor jumped out with Krohn and the others, pulling it up all the way on the rocks. Their feet crunched all around him, boys looked down and picked up the glowing red rocks.

Thor did the same. He grabbed one and held it up, examining it. It sparkled, like a rare jewel in the morning light. He closed his palm and closed his eyes, and a breeze arose as he concentrated. He could feel the rock's power throbbing through his body. Conval was right: this was a magical stone.

He saw the others boys pocketing as many rocks as they could hold, as mementos, and Thor took one and tucked it deep into his pocket. One was enough for him. He didn't need one for himself, and there was only one person he wanted to give one, too: Gwendolyn. That is, if he should ever make it back.

They all began to climb the steep bank, the only entrance leading up the steep cliffs. The mist blew in and out and it was hard to see far, but Thor could make out a narrow path, almost like natural steps, leading up the side of the cliff, covered in moss.

They climbed it single file, Thor slipping as the ocean waves sprayed everything, making the path slick. Thor struggled to keep his balance as a strong gust of wind pounded them.

Finally, they made it to the top. Thor stood on the grassy knoll with the others, at the peak of the dragon's isle, and he looked out. A dark green moss covered the island as far as he could see, and the mist hovered over it. It was a creepy, gloomy place, and as Thor looked out, he suddenly heard a deep roar. It sounded like the earth itself gurgling up, and in the distance, he could see flames and smoke rising in the mist, and disappearing. A strange smell hung in this place, like ash mixed with sulfur. It pervaded everything here. Krohn whined.

Thor swallowed hard. The boys turned and looked at each other, even the bravest of them with fear in their eyes. They had all been through a lot together—but nothing like this. They were really here. It was no longer a drill—it was now life or death.

They all set off as one across the barren wasteland of the isle, walking on the slippery moss, all on guard, all with hands on their swords.

After what felt like hours, the mist swirling all around them, there came a hissing noise, and then a great sound grew, and finally, as the air grew colder, wetter, they reached the edge of a waterfall. Thor looked down over the edge and it seemed to drop forever.

They continued on a trail around the circumference of the waterfall, and headed across a boggy terrain, drenched in spray from the falls, their feet sinking. As they walked and walked, clouds of mist becoming so thick that they could barely see each other, the roar of the dragon came every few minutes, and seemed to grow louder. Thor turned to see where they had come from, but the mist was now too thick to see through. He began to wonder how they would ever make their way back.

As they marched, Reese beside Thor, suddenly Reese lost his footing, and began to fall. Thor used his newfound reflexes to reach out and grab Reese, a moment before he fell. He grabbed him hard by the back of the shirt, and yanked him back. As he stepped forward and looked, he realized that he had just save Reese's life: below them, the ground opened up into what looked like a massive canyon, dropping hundreds of feet below.

Reese turned and looked at Thor with a look of life-saving gratitude.

"I owe you," he said.

Thor shook his head. "No you don't."

The boys all huddled around, looking down at the immense canyon, sinking hundreds of feet into the earth, and wondered.

"What is it?" Elden asked.

"It looks like a canyon," Conval said.

"No," Reese said. "It's not."

"Then what is it?" Conven asked.

"It's a footprint," Reese said.

"A footprint?" Conven asked.

"Look at the indent, how steep it is. And look at that shape, around the edges. That is no canyon, my friend. That is the footprint of the Dragon."

CHAPTER TWENTY TWO

Erec trotted on his horse in the morning light down the well-worn path, flanked by a contingent of the Duke's knights, including his friend Brandt. As they went, heading towards the jousting lanes, they were greeted by thousands of spectators, cheering wildly on both sides of the road.

It had been a long hundred days of jousting, and Erec had won every competition thus far. Today was the final day, everyone out in force to celebrate the finale, and as Erec trotted, he could think only of one thing: Alistair. Her face remained frozen in his mind, and as he tightened his grip on his lance, he knew that he would be fighting for her. If he won today, he could, finally, claim her as his bride. And he was determined that no man, in any province of the kingdom, would defeat him.

As they rode through the immense arched stone gates, into the arena, they were greeted by a cheer from thousands more spectators, seated in the outdoor stone coliseum, looking down at the jousting field in its center. People rose to their feet, throwing down flowers as Erec entered. He felt a swell of pride. He had devoted his life to his fighting skills, and in moments like this, when everyone cheered for him, he felt that all of his hard work paid off. Erec had been defeated by no man in battle.

186

The crowd roared as he trotted in, and he proceeded down the center of the lanes, where he turned and bowed his head to the Duke, who stood with the crowd, flanked by his contingent of soldiers. The Duke bowed back, a smile on his face, and Erec turned and headed to the sideline. All along the sideline were small contingents of knights, hundreds of them, all wearing different armor, of different shapes and colors, riding on a broad array of horses, wielding exotic weapons. They had assembled from all corners of the Ring, each group more exotic than the next. They had been training all year for this, and the competition had been formidable. But Erec had consistently bested them all, and as he thought of Alistair, he knew he would find a way to win today.

Erec waited and watched as a horn sounded, and out charged two knights, from opposing sides of the stadium, one in dark green armor, the other in bright yellow, each holding out their lances as they charged for each other. The green one knocked the yellow off his horse, and the crowd cheered wildly.

Joust after joust ensued, and more and more knights got eliminated. Erec, being the champion, was given the honor of the last spot of the first round.

When the horn sounded he charged without a moment's hesitation. He was matched against one of the best opposing knights—a burly man with black armor, with a chest twice as broad as Erec's. He charged on a horse that wore an awful sneer, and the man's lance seemed twice as long as Erec's.

But Erec, being the professional that he was, did not allow it to faze him. He focused on the man's breastplate, the angle of his head, on the way his armor shifted between the plates. He identified the weak spot immediately, in the way the man lowered his left shoulder. Erec waited until the last moment, aimed his lance at just the right spot, and held it until they clashed.

A gasp spread through the crowd as the opposing knight went flying off his horse, landing on the ground in a clang of metal.

The crowd roared in delight, and Erec rode to the other side of the stadium, and waited his turn for the second round. Dozens of rounds remained.

The day grew long. One after the next, round after round, knights fought, until there were but a handful of warriors left. When they reached the final ten a horn sounded, and a break was called, as the Duke walked out into the middle to address his people. Erec used the opportunity, as did the others, to lift his armor, remove his helmet, and breathe hard. A squire appeared with a bucket of water, and Erec drank some and tipped the rest onto his head and beard. Even though it was now Fall, he was dripping with sweat, breathing hard from hours of fighting. He already felt sore, but as he looked around at the other knights, he could tell they were more tired than he. They did not have the training that he did. He had made a point to train every day of his life, and had never missed a day. He was prepared to be exhausted. These men were not.

The Duke raised both arms to the crowd, and slowly, it quieted down.

"My fellow people," the Duke yelled out. "Our provinces have sent their best and brightest from all corners of the Ring to compete these hundred days for the best and most beautiful bride our kingdom has to offer. Each warrior here has chosen one woman, and whoever wins today, shall have the right to wed that woman, if she agrees. For these final knights, the bout will switch from jousting to handheld fighting. Each warrior will choose one weapon, and they will all fight each other. There will be no killing—but everything else goes. The last man standing wins. Warriors, good luck!" he shouted as he walked off, the crowd roaring behind him.

Erec put his helmet back on, and looked over the weapons cart his squire had rolled to him. He already knew what weapon he wanted: it sat in his waist. He pulled out his old, trusted mace, with its well-worn wooden staff about two feet long, and at its end a spiked metal ball. He had wielded it since his days in the Legion, and he knew no weapon better.

A horn sounded, and suddenly, the ten men charged each other, meeting in the center of the ring.

A large knight, not wearing a helmet, with light blue eyes and a bright blonde beard, a head taller than Erec, charged right for him. He swung a massive club right for Erec's head, with a speed that surprised him.

Erec ducked at the last second, and the club went flying by.

Erec used the opportunity to spin around and crack the man hard in the back of the head with the wooden shaft of his mace, sparing him the metal ball so as not to kill him. The man stumbled and fell, unconscious—and he was the first man down.

The crowd roared.

All around Erec knights fought, and more than one singled him out. Clearly, he was seen as the man to beat, and he ducked and weaved, as one came at him with an axe, another with a halberd, and a third with a spear. So much for the Duke's exhortation not to try to kill each other, Erec thought. Clearly, these knights didn't care.

Erec found himself spinning and twisting, fighting one after the other. One jabbed at him with a long, studded halberd and Erec yanked it from his foe's hands and used it to jab his attacker right at the base of his neck with the wooden end, finding the weak spot above his armor and knocking him down flat on his back.

Erec then spun around and swung the sharp end of the halberd, chopping a spear in half right before it hit him.

He then spun again, drew his mace, and knocked a dagger from the hand of another attacker. He turned the mace sideways and smashed his attacker on the bridge of the nose with the wooden end, breaking his nose and knocking him to the ground.

Another knight charged with a hammer, Erec ducked low and punched him in the solo plexus with his gauntlet. The knight keeled over, dropping his hammer mid-swing.

Just one knight remained now opposite Erec, and the crowd jumped to its feet, cheering like mad, as they circled each other slowly. They were each breathing hard. All around them lay the unconscious bodies of the others who did not make it.

This final knight was from a province Erec did not recognize, wearing a bright red armor with spikes protruding from it, like a porcupine. He held a weapon that resembled a pitchfork, with three long prongs, painted a strange color that shimmered in the light and confused Erec. He jabbed it continually at the air, and it was hard for Erec to focus.

Suddenly he lunged, thrusting it, and Erec blocked the blow at the last second with his mace. The two of them locked in mid-air, pushing back and forth in a tug-of-war. Erec slipped on the blood of one of his opponents, and lost his footing.

Erec fell on his back, and his challenger wasted no time. He thrust his pitchfork right down for Erec's face; Erec blocked it and held it back with the end of his mace. He managed to hold it at bay, but he was losing ground quickly.

The crowd gasped.

"YIELD!" the opponent screamed down.

Erec lay there, struggling, losing steam, when he saw Alistair's face in his mind. He saw her expression when she looked into his eyes, when she asked him to win. And suddenly, he felt overcome with a new strength. He could not let himself lose. Not here. Not today.

With one final burst of strength, Erec rolled out of the way, pulling the pitchfork down and plunging it into the earth beside him. He rolled again and kicked the knight hard in the stomach. The knight fell to his knees, and Erec jumped to his feet and kicked him again, knocking him to his back.

The crowd roared.

Erec drew his dagger, knelt, and held it to the knight's throat. He pushed the tip firmly against it, until the knight understood.

"I YIELD!" the knight yelled.

The crowd roared and screamed in delight.

Erec slowly stood, breathing hard.

He now had but one thing left on his mind.

Alistair.

CHAPTER TWENTY THREE

Thor looked down in awe at the dragon's footprint, sinking hundreds of feet into the earth, the size of a canyon. As the mist cleared down below, at its bottom, Thor spotted something. It was a cave, at the far end, and inside of it he thought he saw something gleaming. It sparkled, then disappeared in the mist.

"There," Thor said, pointing. "Did you see that?"

The boys all squinted.

"I don't see anything," Elden said.

"I thought it sparkled," Thor said.

"It could be the scepter," Reese said.

All around them, dozens of Legion members appeared out of the mist, and one of them found a way down into the canyon, a steep ledge in the cliff. Thor and the others followed, Krohn with them, and they all began to descend, single file.

As they went the trail became steeper, and Thor soon found himself struggling to hold on for dear life as they descended ever deeper into the footprint of the dragon.

They finally reached the bottom and Thor looked up, wondering how they would ever get out.

Down here the floor was covered in fine, black sand, and as they walked, their feet sank into it. The dragon's roar hadn't come in a while, and all was eerily quiet. They were all on guard as they went, crossing the floor of the canyon towards the entrance to the cave. The mist cleared, and it became visible again.

"There!" Thor exclaimed.

The others saw it this time, a gleaming coming from inside.

"I see it," Reese said.

They all proceeded towards the cave, the mist returning, and as they went, Thor had an increasingly ominous feeling. He could not help but feel as if they were being watched, as if they were heading deeper and deeper into the dragon's lair. He hoped and prayed that they could find the scepter and get out of their quick.

Thor suddenly heard a familiar screeching noise, and he turned and craned his neck to the skies: there, flying high above, he was thrilled to see Ephistopheles. He hadn't seen her in he hadn't know how long. He wondered what she was doing here now. He could not help but feel as if she were warning him.

She screeched again, soaring in circles.

As the large group of Legion members converged on the cave, Thor turned and led the way. The world became black as they entered it, long icicles hanging from the ceiling, the sound of water dripping, of bats fluttering. As they walked inside, deeper and deeper, their voices reverberated, the whispers of Legion members on-edge. The only thing illuminating the cave was a sparkling light, not too far from the entrance, of a single object.

As the mist cleared, Thor finally saw what it was—and they all gasped.

There, sticking up from the ground, was the golden scepter. About three feet long, it shined and sparkled, casting off a light so bright it lit up most of the cave through the mist. All the legion members stopped in their tracks, clearly in awe. Thor could feel an intense energy radiating off of it, even from here.

"You saw it first," Reese said to Thor. "You take it. Bring it back for the Legion."

Thor stepped forward, the others following close behind, and knew he should feel relieved. They had found it. Now they could return. But for some reason, as he headed deeper into the cave, he felt more and more on edge. His senses kicked in, and some part of him he didn't understand screamed to him that they were heading deeper into danger.

But with all the boys watching him, he could hardly turn back. He walked forward, reached out, and grabbed the scepter. He felt an electric thrill race through him as he clasped it. It was the most beautiful and powerful thing he had ever touched.

They all turned, hurried out from the cave, the boys crowding around Thor, getting a good look at it. There was relief in the air: their mission was over. Now they could go home. As one, the group shuffled outside the cave, prepared to leave this place.

But the moment they all stepped outside, their world changed. Out of nowhere, a horrific roar rose up, and as they all looked up, Thor saw the most terrifying sight of his life.

The dragon. It raised its head above the canyon, and glared down at them, and Thor had to wonder if this was real or just a nightmare. He had never seen a real dragon before—and he never thought he would live to see one. It was the largest and most terrifying thing he'd ever laid eyes upon. As it raised its long neck, its huge head towering over them, it blocked out the sun, casting a shadow over them all. Just one of its scales was bigger than Thor—and it was covered in thousands of them, reddish-green. It raised its two front legs, each as big as fifty men, and Thor could see its huge claws, three on each foot, reaching out to the heavens, each as sharp as a sword and as long as a tree.

Most terrifying of all, though, was its face, with its long, extended narrow jaw, and behind its open mouth, its rows and rows of teeth, each as large as a house, sharper than any weapon he had ever seen.

It threw its head back and roared, and the sound was enough to split a man in two.

Every single Legion member raised his hands to his ears, and Thor did the same, still clutching the scepter. The ground shook, and Thor felt as if his head would explode. Krohn whined and snarled.

When the dragon finished its roar, it lowered its head, pulled back its throat, opened its mouth and breathed.

Fire came hailing down like a tornado, singing the side of the canyon wall. As the dragon moved its neck, the fire spread—and that was when Thor heard the screams.

Several Legion members screamed out in horrific pain as Thor watched them get burned alive.

Thor watched helplessly, before turning and sprinting with the rest of the boys, running for their lives.

The dragon lowered a leg, and as its foot met the ground, it left another canyon-sized hole, shaking the earth so much that Thor and the Legion members were thrown into the air, a good ten feet. Thor landed hard on his side, and rolled several times.

Thor scurried to his feet and looked up, and saw the dragon getting closer as the rest of the boys ran. Some of the older boys broke into action. One of them, who had carried with him a long rope and grappling hook, distributed the ropes to several others, and soon, the group ran in circles around it, looping the ropes around its legs, trying to trip it up.

It was a valiant effort, and the boys moved quickly and fearlessly, managed to wrap the rope tightly around its legs twice, to Thor's surprise. They expected the dragon to trip and fall as it took its next step.

But they were all horrified as the dragon merely looked down, noticed the rope, and snapped it like it didn't exist. Then it raised a foot and brought it down, crushing several of the older boys into the earth as it did. It swiped with its claws and sliced other boys in half.

Thor watched in horror as O'Connor got hit in the swipe; he missed its claw, but the dragon's foot still sent O'Connor flying through the air and smashing into the canyon wall. Thor prayed he wasn't dead.

The other boys began to flee again, all their options exhausted, and Thor knew he had to do something quickly. At this rate, they would all be dead in minutes. There was no way out of this canyon, and the dragon had them trapped.

As everyone around him continued to run, Thor mustered his courage, and stopped. He stood there, in the center of the canyon floor, and turned and faced the dragon. His heart was pounding, and he knew this might mean his death—but he had to do this.

Thor tried to muster everything that Argon had taught him, tried to summon his spiritual power, whatever power he had. If he had any innate power, he knew that now was the time to draw on it. Now was the time he needed it most.

The dragon suddenly stopped and focused on Thor. It threw back its head and roared, as if furious at being challenged, and in that moment Thor wished that he had ran with the others.

As he stood there alone, facing the dragon, Thor raised one palm, determined to use whatever supernatural powers he had to combat the beast.

Please, God. Please.

The dragon pulled back its throat, opened its mouth, and shot flames right down at Thor.

Thor kept his palm out, hoping and praying that this would work.

As the flames came down, showering down all around him, Thor was stunned to see that his palm created an energy shield around him. The flames harmlessly parted ways around his hand, leaving him safe.

The other boys stopped and watched.

The dragon was enraged. It lifted a foot and brought it down, preparing to crush Thor.

But Thor kept his palm out, and as the foot came down, he was able to use his energy force to stop it with his hand, the foot hovering in mid-air several feet above Thor.

Thor could feel the energy of the beast, feel its strength, its intense desire to kill him. Thor's entire body was shaking as he used all he had to keep it at bay. But he could not hold it back much longer.

Finally, Thor, unable to hold it any longer, released the energy shield and ran. As he did, the foot came crashing down, missing him by feet, plunging into the earth.

The dragon roared, enraged.

The other Legion members stopped and watched, in awe.

The dragon, madder than ever, charged Thor. It dove right for him, opening its rows of teeth, aiming to swallow him whole.

Thor felt a heat rising within himself, and he summoned his energy again. This time he used it to jump—higher than he ever had—and as the dragon ducked down, Thor leapt over its head and landed on its back.

Thor grabbed onto its scales, hanging on for dear life as the dragon bucked. It was like riding a mountain. Thor could sense the dragon's energy and it was the most powerful thing he had ever felt. Thor used his power to try to direct the dragon's energy. He implanted the image in the dragon's mind of flying away.

And that was exactly what the dragon did.

The dragon suddenly lifted up and flew out of the canyon. Thor controlled its mind as it continued to fly, farther and farther away. Thor hung on for dear life, the wind and the mist whipping his face as they climbed higher and higher, flew faster and faster. Soon, the ground was just a speck below them.

Thor directed the dragon to turn over the sea, and they continued to fly. Thor whispered to the dragon to dip down, close to the shore, praying that it would.

It did. As soon as they flew over the shore, Thor took the opportunity. He held his breath and jumped off the dragon's back, hurling through the air, hoping he made it.

He landed in the waves, chest deep in the churning sea. He surfaced, gasping, and turned to watch as the dragon flew away, over the sea, farther and farther away.

With Thor's last ounce of strength, he waded to the shore, and collapsed on the sand, unable to move another inch. He was still clutching the scepter. He could not believe it.

He had made it.

CHAPTER TWENTY FOUR

Andronicus sat on his throne, surrounded by a dozen servant girls, chained naked to the floor, fanning him, placing fruit into his mouth, as he leaned back with a smile and watched the festivities unfold before him. In the circular floor of his massive throne room, the night's games were beginning.

Spread throughout the room were hundreds of Andronicus' closest followers, contingents that had arrived to pay homage from every corner of the Empire, wearing every possible color. They feasted, dancing, drinking, drugging in this room, as they had night after night. There was a never-ending stream of dignitaries who wanted to pay tribute to him. If they did not, he would have his armies crush them in an instant. And these games, the center of the night's festivities, were a nice complement to a long day of drinking and feasting.

The first game of the night was always the most exciting, and this promised to be no exception. They had found a massive Spokebull, with three horns, a jaw twice as wide, eight sets of long fangs, and they had paired it against a Livara—a massive, lion-like creature with four sets of wings. In the ring, the Spokebull charged the Livara, roaring, and the Livara charged back. It promised to be a good matchup.

The two creatures, each enraged, met in the middle, snarling, each sinking its fangs into the other's hide. They hit the ground and rolled, and the room became filled with the sounds of their vicious snarls. Within moments, blood and saliva was spraying all over the room. Andronicus smiled wide, thrilled as some of the blood sprayed through the gate and hit him in the face. Inspired, he reached over, slipped one hand around one of the naked girls, and pulled her up onto his lap. Before she knew what was happening, he extended his huge fangs, and plunged them into her throat.

She shrieked as he drank her blood, feeling the hot liquid gush down his throat, holding her tight until she finally stopped writhing. Finally, she slumped there, dead, in his arms, and he wiped the back of his mouth, and let her lie there. There were few things he enjoyed more than holding a freshly-dead corpse in his lap. This was turning out to be a great night, indeed.

An agonizing howl rang out, and the crowd jumped to its feet, roaring, as one of the animals got the best of the other. Andronicus stood himself, and looked down to see that the spoke-bull had won, piercing the Livara's chest with his third horn. It stood over it, snorting, tapping its foot.

The crowd cheered as an attendant opened the gate, preparing for the next bout.

As he did, though, something went wrong: the spoke-bull, enraged, charged right for the attendant. The man could not get out of the way quickly enough, and the animal gouged him with its horns, piercing his stomach and sending him up high over his head, pinning him to the cage of the arena. Instead of rushing to help him, the crowd screamed in delight, as the attendant hung there in agony. No one came to his help; on the contrary, they all enjoyed it.

Three more attendants rushed in, holding spears, and they kept the beast at bay as they went to rescue their co-worker. The beast charged them, biting their spears and breaking them—until finally another attendant stepped forward with a huge double axe, and in one clean swoop, chopped off its head. Its corpse fell to the side, blood gushing everywhere, and the crowd roared in excitement.

Several more attendants rushed in to clean up the bloody mess, and a door opened from another end of the arena and two more animals were led in for the next round. They were identical. They looked like rhinoceroses, but were three times the size, and one was led to each end of the ring, grunting and snarling, barely able to be contained by four attendants with ropes.

As the cadavers were pulled out and the gate barely closed, a whistle sounded, and the two animals were released from their ropes. Without hesitating, they charged each other, ramming heads as they met in the middle. There was an awful crash as their heads met, their hides as hard as iron, shaking the entire room.

The crowd cheered in delight.

Andronicus slowly sat back down, still holding the fresh corpse in his lap, reveling in the games. They were going even better tonight than he had expected, and his spirits had not been this high in he did not know how long.

"My liege, forgive me," came a voice.

Andronicus turned to see one of his messengers standing beside them, whispering in his ear.

"Forgive my interruption, master, but I bring important news."

"Speak it then," Andronicus snarled, still looking straight ahead, trying to ignore the man. Andronicus had a sinking feeling that whatever it was would interrupt his mood. And he did not want it interrupted.

"News has spread that the McCloud army has invaded the other half of the Ring. Our spies tell us that the MacGil's kingdom may be overrun within days, and that the McClouds will control the Ring."

Andronicus slowly nodded, taking in the information with a seething rage that he did not show—then he reached over, grabbed the messenger with both hands, stood, and hoisted him across the room with a superhuman strength. The messenger, a small, frail man from the Hinterlands, went flying through the air, shrieking, and the crowd watched, transfixed, as he cleared the fence to the arena and landed inside with the wild animals.

The two animals, startled, took a break from smashing into each other and turned towards the messenger. Together, they charged him, and the messenger turned and ran, screaming, trying to flee. But there was nowhere for him to go. As he climbed the wall, trying to get out, one of the animals pierced his back with its thick horn, pinning him to the cage.

The messenger shrieked, blood gushing from his mouth, grasping the wall with his fingernails as he died.

The crowd rose to its feet, screaming in delight.

Andronicus pondered the news. It had put him in a very bad mood, indeed. That McCloud king had defied him, had not accepted his offer, had not acceded to his wishes to let him cross the canyon, to attack the MacGils together. That McCloud king was more hard-headed than Andronicus had anticipated. He was out of Andronicus's reach. And Andronicus hated things he could not control.

Andronicus had expected a moment like this. The Ring had been nothing but a thorn in his side, in the side of the entire Empire—the only free territory left in it, for as long as his ancestors could remember. He was determined to change that. He had conquered virtually every corner of the Empire, and his victory could not be complete without invading the Ring, making the entire land subservient to his will.

Andronicus had a backup scenario in mind for news such as this, and now it was time to employ it.

He suddenly rose, the entire room dropping to its knees and bowing down as he did, and threw off the lifeless corpse, now cold, of the young girl. He marched across the room, as hundreds of his followers bowed low to the ground, and was followed his entourage of loyal advisors. The advisors knew better than to question where he was going, knowing to obediently follow until he told them otherwise.

Andronicus left the chamber, and his men followed close as he entered the corridors of his castle.

Andronicus marched, fuming with rage, deep into the bowels of his castle, working his way down towards the torture chambers. The corridors were shaped in wide circles, and he went around and around, the walls lined with torches, until finally he reached a square, metal door, iron spikes protruding from it. At the sight of him, three attendants hurried to yank it open, bowing their heads low.

Andronicus marched in, his men close behind.

In the chamber stood two prisoners, members of the McCloud kingdom, men they had captured years ago off of one of the McCloud ships. Andronicus examined the men, chained against the opposite wall, hands and feet bound, and decided that they looked ripe. They had kept these men chained here for years, starving them, torturing them once a day, breaking them utterly, completely, for a moment such as this. For a moment when McCloud had defied him. Now it was time for Andronicus to use them, to extract the information he had been needing to know for a lifetime. He only one had shot at this, and he needed to get it right.

Andronicus stepped forward, grabbed a long, sharp hook off the wall, came up close to one of the men, and held the hook under his chin. He began to lift it, under the most tender and fragile part of his vocal cords, until the point pierced the skin.

The man's eyes flooded with tears, and he shrieked out in agony.

"What is it that you want?" the man shrieked.

Andronicus smiled down at him.

"The Canyon," he growled, slowly. "You have one chance to give me the answer. How do we breach it. What is its secret? What is the energy shield? Who controls it?"

The man blinked several times, sweating.

"I don't know," he said. "I swear it—"

Andronicus was not in the mood: he lifted the weapon high and the man shrieked in agony as it severed his throat, then his head. A moment later, his head rolled off his body, onto the floor.

Andronicus turned and looked at the other prisoner, chained to the opposite wall, the other McCloud. The man blinked several times, staring; he started moaning and shaking as Andronicus approached with the hook.

"Please!" the man squealed, "please, don't kill me! Please, I beg you!"

McCloud got close to him, and held the hook to his throat, leaning in.

"You know the question," Andronicus said. "Answer if you choose. If not, join your friend. You have three seconds. One, two—"

He began to lift the hook.

"Okay!" the man screamed. "Okay! I will tell you! I will tell you everything!"

Andronicus stared at him closely, trying to see if he was lying. He was expert at that, having killed so many people in his lifetime. As he stared deeply into the man's pupils, dilating, he saw that he was telling the truth.

Slowly, he smiled, relaxed. Finally, the Ring would be his.

CHAPTER TWENTY FIVE

Gwendolyn stood on the upper parapet of the castle on the cold Fall day, the wind blowing back her hair, and looked out at the brilliant countryside. The rolling farmlands were filled fall harvesters, dozens of women gathering fruits into baskets. All around her, everything was changing, all the leaves a myriad of colors, purples and greens and oranges and yellows…. The two suns were changing, too, as they always did in the Fall, now casting a yellow and purple hue to the day. It was a magnificent day, and looking out at the vista before her, everything seemed right in the world.

For the first time since her father's death, she felt a sense of optimism. She had awakened before the dawn, and had waited with anticipation the tolling of the bells, announcing the return of the Legion. She waited and watched the horizon for hours, and below her, as the day broke, she could see crowds already beginning to form in the streets below, preparing for the parades to welcome them back.

Gwen was overjoyed with excitement. Today was the day Thor would return to her.

She had been up all night, counting the minutes till sunrise. She could hardly believe it had finally come. Today, Thor was returning. All would be right again in the world.

She also felt a sense of joy, of accomplishment, that Kendrick had not been executed. Somehow, her meeting had gotten through to her mother. She hated the idea of his wallowing in the dungeon, and every day she thought of ways to get him out, but for now, at least she had kept him alive.

She was determined to prove who murdered her father, but had been unable over the last hundred days, despite her efforts, to find any new leads. Godfrey, too, had reached a dead end. They were both blocked at every turn. Gwendolyn felt increasingly threatened under Gareth's watchful eye, his multitude of spies; she felt less safe in the castle as days went by. She winced as she thought of the scar Gareth's assassin had left on her cheek; it was light, hard to see except in direct sunlight, looking more like a scratch—but nonetheless, it was there. Every time she looked in the mirror, she saw it, and she remembered. She knew she had to make a change, and make one soon. Gareth was becoming more unhinged with each passing day, and there was no telling what he might do.

But now that Thor was returning, now that the Legion would be home, including her younger brother Reese, she no longer felt so alone with all of this. Change was in the air, and the status quo would not remain the same. She felt it would only be a matter of time until she found a way to release her brother. And most importantly, she could now be with Thor permanently. She had not spoken to her mother since that last fateful meeting, and she suspected she would not talk to her again; yet at least she was no longer an obstacle between her and Thor.

Gwen watched the horizon. In the far distance, beyond the Canyon, she saw the faintest glimmer of the ocean, and looked for any signs of sails. She knew it was overly optimistic to be able to spot them from this far away, and even once they landed, they were still a half day's ride away. But she could not help but watch. All around her, the bells tolled. She had worn her finest white silks for the day. A part of her wanted Thor to take her away from here, from all this, from all this castle maneuvering, to a place where they could be safe. To have a new life somewhere. With him. She did not know what or where. But she knew she needed to start again.

"Gwendolyn?" came a voice.

She spun, jolted from her thoughts, and to her surprise saw a man standing there, a few feet away. He had snuck up on her, and worse, it was a man that she despised. Not a man—a boy.

Alton. The very face of duplicity, of aristocracy, of everything wrong with this place.

He stood there, looking so arrogant, so self-assured, dressed in his silly outfit, wearing an ascot even in the fall, and she despised him more than ever. She was everything he hated in a man. She was still furious at him for misleading her, for telling her all those lies about Thor that nearly broke them apart. He had made a fool of her. She had vowed to never set eyes on him again—not that she liked him to begin with.

Thus far she had been successful. Months had passed since she had seen him last, and she could

210

not believe he had the audacity to come out of the woodwork now, to be standing here. She wondered how he'd even got up here, how he slipped past the guards. He must have used his nonsense line about being royalty, and they must have believed it. He could be very convincing, even in his lies.

"What are you doing here?" she demanded.

He took a step closer to her, one step too close for her. There were only a few feet in between them, and she felt her body tense up.

He smiled, as if not detecting her hostility.

"I've come to give you a second chance," he said.

She laughed aloud at his absurdity.

"*Me*? A second chance?" she asked, incredulous. "As if I ever wanted a first chance to begin with. And who are *you* to be giving anyone chances? If anything, it would be I giving *you* a second chance. But as I said, there are no chances. You're nothing to me. You never were. You never seem to accept that. You live in a world of delusion."

He snorted back at her.

"I understand that when a woman's feelings are so strong for man, she can sometimes live in denial, so I forgive you your rash words. You know that you and I have always been meant to be, from the time we were children. You can try to resist it, but you know as well as I do that nothing will tear us apart."

She laughed.

"Tear us apart?" she mocked. "You really are sick. We were never together. We will *never* be together. There is nothing to tear apart. Except for your lies. How dare you lie to me about Thor!" she yelled, her voice rising, growing indignant.

Alton merely shrugged.

"Technicalities," he said. "He is a commoner. Who cares about him?"

"I care—very much. You spouted lies about him and made a fool of me."

"If I took liberty with the facts, it makes no difference. If he's not guilty of one voice, surely he will be of another. The fact is, he is a commoner and beneath you, and you know I'm right. He will never be good enough for you.

"I, on the other hand, am ready to accept you as my wife. I've come to you to confirm that you want me to make arrangements before I do. After all, weddings are expensive. My family is going to pay for it."

Gwen looked back at him in disbelief. She'd never met anyone so out of touch with reality, so pompous. She could not believe that he actually seemed genuine. It made her sick.

"I don't know how many ways I can tell you, Alton: I have no love for you. I don't even have any like for you. In fact, I have the utmost hatred. And I always will. So I suggest you leave me now. I would never marry you. I would never even be your friend. Besides, I have other plans."

Alton smiled, undeterred.

"If by that you mean your supposed marriage to Thor, you can think again," he said, confidently, a mischievous smile at his lips.

Gwen felt her blood run cold.

"What are you talking about?" she hissed.

Alton stood there, smiling, reveling in the moment.

"Your lover boy Thor is not returning. I have it on good source he will be killed on the Isle of Mist. Quite a fatal accident, I'm afraid. So you can stop pining for his return home. It won't happen."

Gwen saw the confidence in his face, and she felt her heart crash. Was he telling the truth? If so, she wanted to kill him with her on their hands.

Alton took a step forward, staring into her eyes.

"So you see Gwendolyn, destiny is meant for the two of us after all. Stop resisting it. Take my hand now, and let's make matters official. Let's stop fighting what we already know to be true."

Alton held out a hand, his smile widening as he stared at her. But she could also see drops of sweat forming on his forehead in the sun.

"Still no response?" he said. "Then allow me to add one more point," he added, as he held his hand out there, trembling. "I've heard it on good rumor that your family plans to marry you off soon, like your older sister. After all, they can't afford to have an unwed MacGil roaming around. You can choose my hand now in marriage—or if not, allow yourself to be assigned to some stranger. And I might add that it might be a brutal stranger, a savage from some corner of the Ring. You'd do far better with someone like me, someone you know."

"You lie," Gwen spat, feeling her entire body tremble. "I cannot be married off. Not by my family. Not by anyone."

"Oh can't you? Your sister was."

"That was when my father was alive. When he was King."

"And do we not have a King now?" he asked with a wry smile. "The King's law is the King's law."

Gwen's heart was racing as she contemplated his words. Gareth? Her brother? Marry her off? Could he be so sick, so cruel? Did he even have the right to do so? After all, he may be king, but he was not her father.

She did not want to ponder any of this anymore. She was revolted by Alton. She had no idea what to believe. She took a step closer to him, and put on her firmest face.

"Let me make it as clear for you as I can," she enunciated slowly, her voice as cold as steel. "If you come near me again, I will have the royal guards— the royal guards of the *true* royal family—imprison you. They will throw you in the dungeon and you will never get out again. I can guarantee you that. Now get out of my presence, once and for all."

Alton stood there, staring, and slowly his smile collapsed into a frown. Eventually his face started to tremble, and she could see his face change, boil over with rage.

"Don't forget," he hissed, "you've brought this on yourself."

She had never heard him so angry before, as he spun on his heel, stormed off the parapets, and down the steps.

She stood there, alone, trembling inside, listening to his footsteps disappear for a very long time. She prayed to the gods that she never see him again.

Gwen turned back to the parapets, walked to the edge and looked out. Was anything he said true? She prayed not. That was the problem with Alton—he had a way of implanting the worst thoughts in her head, thoughts she could not get out.

She closed her eyes and tried to shake the memory. He was an awful creature, the epitome of everything she hated about this place, the epitome of everything she felt was wrong with the world.

She opened her eyes, looked out over King's court, and tried to make it all disappear. She tried to get back to the place she had been before Alton had appeared, to thinking of Thor, of his arrival home today, of being back in his arms. If anything, seeing Alton just made her realize how much she loved Thor. Thor was the opposite of Alton in every way: he was a noble, proud warrior, with a pure heart. He was more royal than Alton would ever be.

It made her realize how much she wanted to be with Thor, how she would do anything for it to be just the two of them, far away from this place. And she felt more determined than ever to let nothing come between them.

But as Gwen stood there, trying to recapture her peace, to picture Thor's face, the shape of his jaw, the color of his eyes, the curve of his lips, she could not. Anger burned in her veins. Her peace had been shattered. She could not think clearly anymore, and she wanted to think clearly, before Thor arrived.

Gwen turned on her heel and crossed the parapet, leaving the roof, entering the spiral staircase, and beginning her descent. She needed a change of environment. She would enter the royal gardens, and take a long walk amidst the flowers. That would change her mindset—it always did.

As she descended, going down flight after flight, traveling the well-worn stone staircase that she had since a child, something felt wrong. She felt it before she saw it. It was a chill, a cold energy, like a sudden cloud passing over her.

Then she saw it, out of the corner of her eye. Motion, darkness. A blur. It all happened so quickly.

And then she felt it.

Gwen was tackled from behind, coarse hands grabbing her around the waist, driving her down to the ground.

She hit the stone hard, tumbling down the steps flight after flight.

The world spun, was a blur, as she banged and scraped her knees, her elbows, her forearms. She instinctively covered her head as she rolled, the way her instructors had taught her when she was a child, and shielded her head from the worst of it.

After several steps, she did not know how many, she rolled onto a plateau, on one of the corridors leading off the stairwell. She lay there curled up in a ball and breathed hard, trying to catch her breath, the wind knocked out of her.

There was no time to rest. She heard footsteps, coming down, fast, too fast, big heavy footsteps, and knew that her attacker, whoever he was, was right on her heels. She willed her body to get up, to regain her feet, and it took every ounce of energy that she had.

Somehow, she managed to get to her hands and knees, just as he came into view. It was Gareth's dog, back again. This time he wore a single leather glove, it's knuckles covered in metal spikes.

Gwen quickly reached down to her waist and pulled out the weapon that Godfrey had given her. She pulled back the wooden sheath, revealing the blade, and lunged for him. She was quick—quicker than she imagined she could be, and aimed the blade right for his heart.

But he was even quicker than she. He swatted her wrist, and the small blade went flying, landing on the stone floor and skidding across it.

Gwen turned and watched it fly, and felt all her hopes go flying with it. Now, she was defenseless.

Gareth's dog wound up with his fist, with the metal knuckles, and swung right for her face. It all happened too fast for her to react. She saw the knuckles, the metal spikes, coming down right for her cheek—and she knew that in just a moment they would all puncture her face, and leave her horribly, permanently, scarred. Disfigured. She closed her eyes and braced herself for the life-changing pain that would follow.

Suddenly there came a noise, and to her surprise, her attacker's blow stopped in mid-air, just inches from her cheek. It was a clanging noise, and she looked over to see a man standing beside her, a wide man, with a hunched, twisted back, holding up a short metal staff. It was inches from her face, and the staff blocked the blow of the man's fist.

Steffen. He had saved her from the blow. But what was he doing here?

Steffen held his staff there with a trembling hand, holding back the attacker's fist, preventing

Gwen from being injured. He then leaned forward with his metal staff and jabbed the man hard, right in the face. The blow broke his nose and sent him plunging down to the cold stone floor, on his back.

Gareth's dog lay there, defenseless, and Steffen stood over him, holding his staff, looking down at him.

Steffen turned for a moment and looked at Gwen, concern in his eyes.

"Are you okay, my lady?" he asked.

"Look out!" Gwen yelled.

Steffen turned back, but it was too late. He had taken his eyes off of Gareth's dog a moment too long, and being the tricky assassin that he was, reached up and swept Steffen, kicking him behind the knee and sending him flying flat on his back.

The metal staff went clanging on the stone, rolling across the corridor, as the man jumped on top of Steffen and pinned him down. He reached over, grabbed Gwen's blade off the floor, raised it high, and in one quick motion, brought it down for Steffen's throat.

"Meet your maker, you deformed waste of creation," the man snarled.

But as he brought his blade down, there came a horrible groan—and it was not from Steffen. It was from Gareth's dog.

Gwen stood there, hands trembling, hardly believing what she had just done. She hadn't even thought about it, she had just done it—and she looked down as if she were outside of herself. When the iron staff had landed on the floor, she had grabbed it and hit Gareth's dog in the side of the head. She hit him so hard, right before he stabbed Steffen, that she sent him onto the floor, limp. It was a fatal blow, a perfect blow.

He lay there, blood pouring from his head, and his eyes were frozen. Dead.

Gwen looked down at the iron staff in her hands, so heavy, the iron cold, and suddenly dropped it. It hit the stone with a clang. She felt like crying. Steffen had saved her life. And she had saved his.

"My lady?" came a voice.

She looked up and saw Steffen standing there, beside her, looking at her with concern.

"It was my aim to save your life," he said. "But you have saved mine. I owe you a great debt."

He half bowed in acknowledgment.

"I owe you my life," she said. "If it weren't for you, I would be dead. What are you doing here?"

Steffen looked at the ground, then back up at her. This time, he did not avoid her gaze. This time he looked right at her. He was no longer shifting, no longer evasive. He seemed like a different person.

"I sought you out to apologize," he said. "I was lying to you. And your brother. I came to tell you the truth. About your father. I was told you were up this way, and I came here looking for you. I stumbled across your encounter with this man. I'm fortunate that I did."

Gwen looked at Steffen with a whole new sense of gratitude and admiration. She also felt a burning curiosity to know.

She was about to ask him, but this time Steffen needed no prodding.

"A blade did indeed fall down the chute that night," he said. "A dagger. I found it, and took it for myself. I hid it. I don't know why. But I thought it unusual. And valuable. It is not every day something like that falls down. It was thrown into the waste, so I saw no harm in keeping it for myself."

He cleared his throat.

"But as fate would have it, my master beat me that night. He beat me every night, from the time I began working there, for thirty years. He was a cruel, horrific man. I accepted it every night. But that night, I'd had enough. Do you see these lashes on my back?"

He turned and lifted his shirt, and Gwen flinched at the sight: he was covered in lacerations.

Steffen turned back.

"I had reached my limit. And that dagger, it was in my hands. Without thinking, I took my revenge. I defended myself."

He pleaded with her.

"My lady, I am not a murderer. You must believe me."

Her heart went out to him.

"I do believe you," she said, reaching out and clasping his hands.

He looked up, eyes welling with tears of gratitude.

"You do?" he asked, like a little boy.

She nodded back.

"I did not tell you," he added, "because I feared you would have me imprisoned for the death of my master. But you have to understand, it was self-defense. And you promised once that if I told you I would not go to jail."

"And I still do," Gwen said, meaning it. "You shall not go to jail. But you must help me find the owner of that dagger. I need to put my father's killer away."

Steffen reached into his waist, and pulled out an object wrapped in a rag. He reached out and handed it to her, placing it in her palm.

Slowly, she pulled it back, revealing the weapon he had found. As Gwen felt the weight of it in her palm, her heart pounded. She felt a chill. She was holding her father's murder weapon. She wanted to throw it away, get as far away from it as she could.

But at the same time, she was transfixed. She saw the stains on it, saw the hilt. She gingerly turned it over every which way.

"I see no markings on it, my lady," Steffen said. "Nothing that would indicate its owner."

But Gwen had been raised around royal weapons her entire life, and Steffen had not. She knew where to look, and what to look for. She turned it upside down, and looked at the bottom of the hilt. Just in case, just in some off-chance it belonged to a member of the royal family.

As she did, her heart stopped. There were the initials: GAN.

Gareth Andrew MacGil.

It was her brother's knife.

CHAPTER TWENTY SIX

Gwen walked beside Godfrey, her mind reeling from her encounter with Gareth's dog, with Steffen. She could still feel the scrapes on her knees and elbows, and felt traumatized as she thought how close she had come to dying. She also felt traumatized to think that she had just killed a man. Her hands still shook, as she relived her swinging that iron staff again and again.

Yet at the same time, she also felt profoundly grateful to be alive, and profoundly grateful to Steffen for saving her life. She had badly underestimated him, underestimated what a good person he was, regardless of his appearance, his role in his master's murder, which was clearly deserved and self-defense. She was ashamed at herself for judging him based on his appearance. He had found in her a friend for life. When all this was over, she was determined to not let him wallow away in the basement anymore. She was determined to pay him back, to make his life better somehow. He was a tragic character. She would find a way to help him.

Godfrey looked more concerned than ever as the two of them marched down the castle corridors; he had been aghast as she'd recounted to him the story of her near assassination, of Steffen's rescue—and of Steffen's revelation of the dagger. She had brought it to him and Godfrey had examined it, too, and had confirmed it was Gareth's.

Now that they had the murder weapon, the two of them knew instantly what they needed to do: before going to the council with this, they had to get the witness they needed. Godfrey had recalled Firth's involvement, his walking with Gareth on that forest trail, and he figured they needed to corner Firth in first, get him to confess—then, with the murder weapon and a witness, they could bring this to the council and bring down their brother for good. Gwen had agreed, and the two of them had set off to find Firth in the stables, and had been marching ever since.

As they went, Gwen still held the dagger in her hands, the weapon that had murdered her father, still stained with his blood, and she felt like crying. She missed her father terribly, and it pained her beyond words to think that he had died this way, that this weapon had been thrust into him.

But her emotions swung from sadness to rage, as she realized Gareth's role in all of this. This had confirmed her worst suspicions. A part of her had clung to the idea that maybe, after all, Gareth was not as bad as all of this, that maybe he was redeemable. But after this latest attempt on her life, and seeing this murder weapon, she knew that was not the case—he was hopeless. Pure evil. And he was her brother. How did that affect her? After all, she carried his same blood. Did that mean that evil lurked somewhere inside her, too? Could a brother and a sister be so different?

"I still can't conceive that Gareth would do all of this," she said to Godfrey as they walked quickly, side-by-side, twisting their way through the corridors of the castle, heading towards the distant stables.

"Can't you?" Godfrey said. "You know Gareth. The throne has been all he's ever lived for."

"But to kill our father, just for power? Just for a title?"

Godfrey turned and looked at her.

"You are naïve, aren't you? What else is there? What more can someone want than to be king? Than to have that kind of power?"

She looked at him, reddening.

"I think you are the one who is naïve," she said. "There's a great deal more to life than power. In fact, power, ultimately, is the least attractive thing. Do you think our father was happy? He was miserable ruling this kingdom. All he ever did was complain, and pine for more time with us."

Godfrey shrugged.

"You hold an optimistic view of him. He and I didn't get along nearly as well. In my mind's eye, he was as power-hungry as the rest of them. If he wanted to spend time with us, he could have. He chose not to. Besides, I was relieved when he didn't spend time with me. He hated me."

Gwen examined her brother as they walked, and for the first time she realized how different their experience of childhood had been. It was as if he grew up with a different father than she did. She wondered if it was because he was a boy, and she a girl; or if it was just a clash of personalities. As she thought of it, she realized he was right: her father had not been kind to him. She didn't know why she didn't fully realize it before, but as she did, she suddenly felt terrible for Godfrey. She understood now why he spent all his time in the tavern. She had always assumed her father disapproved of Godfrey because he wasted his time in the alehouse. But maybe it was more complex than that. Maybe Godfrey sought out the alehouse to begin with because he was the victim of their father's disapproval.

"You could never win father's approval, could you?" she asked, compassionately, beginning to understand. "So then, after a point, you didn't even bother to try."

Godfrey shrugged, trying to seem nonchalant, but she could see the sadness in his face.

"He and I were different people," he said. "And he could never accept that."

As she studied him, she saw Godfrey in a different light. For the first time, she didn't see him as a slovenly drunk; she saw him as a child with great potential, who was poorly raised. She felt anger at her father for it. In fact, she could even see traces of her father in him.

"I bet that if he treated you differently, you'd be a different person," she said. "I think all of your behavior was just a cry for his attention. If he had just accepted you on your own terms, I think that, of all of us, you would have been the most like him."

Godfrey looked at her, surprised, then looked away. He looked down with a furrowed brow and seemed to ponder that.

They continued walking in silence, opening one door after the other down the long, twisting corridors. Finally, they burst out of the castle, into the cool Fall air. Gwen squinted at the light.

The courtyard was abuzz with activity, the masses excited, bustling to and fro, people drinking in the streets, an early celebration.

"What's happening?" Godfrey asked.

Suddenly, Gwen remembered.

"The Legion returns home today," she answered.

With everything else that had gone on, she had completely forgotten about it. Her heart skipped a beat as she thought again of Thor. His ship would be coming home soon. She ached to see him.

"It will be a huge celebration," Gwen added, joyfully.

Godfrey shrugged.

"They never accepted me into the Legion. Why should I care?"

She looked at him, upset.

"You *should* care," she scolded. "Your brother Reese will be returning home. As will Thor."

Godfrey turned and looked at her.

"You like that common boy, don't you?" he asked.

Gwen blushed, silent.

"I can see why," Godfrey said. "There is something noble to him. Something pure."

Gwen thought about that, and realized it was true. Godfrey was more perceptive than she'd realized.

They marched across the castle grounds, and as they did, Gwen felt the knife burning in her hand, and wanted to throw it as far away from her as she could. She spotted the stables in the distance, and increased their pace. Firth was not far now.

"Gareth will find some way out of this," Godfrey said. "You know that, don't you? He always does."

"Not if we get Firth to admit to it, and to be a witness."

"And even if so, then what?" Godfrey asked. "Do you really think he'll step down from the throne that easily?"

"Of course I don't. But we will force him. We will get the council to force him. With proof, we can summon the guards ourselves."

Godfrey shrugged, skeptical.

"And even if that should work, even if we should depose him—then what? Then who will rule? One of the nobles might rush to fill the power vacuum. Unless one of us rises to the throne."

"Kendrick should rule," Gwen said.

Godfrey shook his head.

"No. *You* must rule. It was father's wish."

Gwen blushed.

"But I don't want to," she said. "That's not why I'm doing this. I just want justice for father."

"You may, after all, get justice for him. But you must also take the throne. To do otherwise would be to disrespect him. And if you say no, then the next eldest legitimate son is me—and I am not going to rule. Never," he insisted firmly.

Gwen's heart pounded as she thought of it. She could think of nothing she wanted less.

They crossed the soft grass of the stable ground, and reached the large open-air entrance to the stables. They headed inside, and it was darker in here, as they walked past rows and rows of horses, each more elegant than the next, prancing and neighing as they went. They walked on a floor of hay, the smell of horses filling Gwen's nose, and continued all the way to the end. They turned down another corridor, then down another, and finally, they came to the place where the King's family kept their horses.

They hurried over to Gareth's corner, saw all of his horses, and Gwen examined the weapons rack against the wall. In the row of daggers, one was missing.

Gwen slowly unwrapped the dagger, gingerly lifted it and placed it in the spot on the wall. It was a perfect fit. She was breathless.

"Bravo," Godfrey said. "But that still doesn't prove that Gareth used this knife—or that he ordered the murder," she said. "He could argue that someone stole it."

"It doesn't prove it," she countered. "But it helps. And with a witness, the case is closed."

Gwen wrapped the knife back in its cloth, stored it back in her waistband, and they continued down the stables until they reached the stable caretaker.

"My liege," he said, looking up in surprise at the presence of two members of the royal family. "What brings you here? Are you here for your horses? We have no notice."

"It's okay," Gwen said, laying an assuring hand on his wrist. "We are not here for our horses. We come on a different matter. We're looking for the stable boy who tends to Gareth's horses. Firth."

"Yes, he's here today. Check around back. In the hay pile."

They hurried down the corridor, out the stables, then went around to the back of the building.

There, in the large, open space, was Firth, using a pitchfork to shovel piles of hay. There seemed to be a sadness on his face.

As they approached, Firth stopped and looked up, and his eyes opened wide in surprise. And something else—perhaps fear.

Gwen could see all that she needed to in that stare. He had something to hide.

"Did Gareth send you?" Firth asked.

Gwen and Godfrey exchanged a glance.

"And why would our brother do that?" Godfrey asked.

"I'm just asking," Firth said.

"No," Gwen said. "He did not. Were you expecting him to?"

Firth narrowed his eyes, looking back and forth to the two of them. He slowly shook his head, then fell silent.

Gwen exchanged a look with Godfrey, then turned back to Firth.

"We've come here on our own," she said. "To ask you some questions about our father's murder."

She watched Firth carefully and could tell he was nervous. He fidgeted with the pitchfork.

"Why would you ask me?"

"Because you know who did it," Godfrey said flatly.

Firth stopped fidgeting and looked at him, real fear in his face. He gulped.

"If I knew that, my lord, it would be treason to hide it. I could be executed for that. So the answer is no. I do now know who did it."

Gwen could see how nervous he was, and she took a step closer to him.

"What are you doing out here, tending hay?" she asked, realizing. "A few months ago, you were always by Gareth's side. In fact, after he became king, he elevated you, if I'm not mistaken."

"He did, my lady," Firth said meekly.

"Then why has he cast you out, relegated you to this? Did you two have a falling out?"

Firth's eyes shifted, and he swallowed, looking from Gwen to Godfrey.

He remained silent, though.

"And what did you two have a falling out about?" Gwen pressed, following her instinct. "I wonder if it had something to do with my father's assassination? Something to do with the cover up, perhaps?"

"We did not have a falling out, my lady. I chose to come and work here."

Godfrey laughed.

"Did you?" Godfrey asked. "You were tired of being in the King's Castle, so you chose instead to come out here and shovel crap in the stables?"

Firth looked away, reddening.

"I will ask you just one more time," Gwen said firmly. "Why did my brother send you here? What did you two argue over?"

Firth cleared his throat.

"Your brother was upset that he was unable to wield the Dynasty Sword. That's all it was. I was a victim of his wrath. It is nothing more, my lady."

Gwen and Godfrey exchanged a look. She sensed there was some truth to that—but that he was hiding something still.

"And what do you know of the missing dagger from Gareth's stable?" Godfrey asked.

Firth swallowed.

"I know nothing of a missing dagger, my Lord."

"Don't you? There are only four on the wall. Where is the fifth?"

"Perhaps Gareth used it for something. Perhaps it is lost?" Firth said weakly.

Gwen and Godfrey exchanged a look.

"It's funny you should say that," Gwen said, "because we just spoke to a certain servant who gave us a different account. He told us about the night of our father's murder. A dagger was thrown down, into the waste pit, and he saved it. Do you recognize it?"

She reached down, unwrapped the knife and showed it to him.

His eyes opened wide, and he looked away.

"Why do you carry that, my lady?"

"It's interesting you should ask," Gwen said, "because the servant told us something else," Gwen lied, bluffing. "He saw the face of the man who threw it down. And it was yours."

Firth's eyes opened wider.

"He has a witness, too," Godfrey added. "They both saw your face."

231

Firth looked so anxious, it looked as if he might crawl out of his skin.

Gwen took a step closer. He was guilty, she could sense it, and she wanted to put him away.

"I will only ask you one last time," she said, her voice made of steel. "Who murdered our father? Was it Gareth?"

Firth gulped, clearly caught.

"Even if I knew something of your father's murder," Firth said, "it would do me no good to speak of it. As I said, the punishment is execution. What would I stand to gain?"

Gwen and Godfrey exchanged a look.

"If you tell us who was responsible for the murder, if you admit that Gareth was behind it, even if you took some part in it, we will see to it that you are pardoned," Gwen said.

Firth looked at her, eyes narrowing.

"A full pardon?" he asked. "Even if I had some role in it?"

"Yes," Gwen answered. "If you agree to stand as witness against our brother, you will be pardoned. Even if you are the one who wielded the knife. After all, our brother is the one who stood to gain from the murder, not you. You were just his lackey.

"So now tell us," Gwen insisted. "This is your last chance. We already have proof linking you to the murder. If you remain silent, you will certainly wallow in prison for the rest of your life. The choice is yours."

As she spoke, Gwen felt a strength rising through her, the strength of her father. The strength of justice. In that moment, for the first time, she actually felt like she might be able to rule.

Firth stared back for a long time, looking back and forth between Gwen and Godfrey, clearly debating.

Then, finally, Firth burst into tears.

"I thought it was what your brother wanted," he said, crying. "He put me up to getting the poison. That was his first attempt. When it failed, I just thought…well… I just thought I would finish the job for him. I held no ill will against your father. I swear. I'm sorry. I was just trying to please Gareth. He wanted it so badly. When he failed, I couldn't stand to see it. I'm sorry," he said, weeping, collapsing on the ground, sitting there, hands on his head.

Godfrey, to Gwen's surprise, rushed over, grabbed Firth roughly by the shirt, and yanked him to his feet. He held him tight, scowling down at him.

"You little shit," he said. "I should kill you myself."

Gwen was surprised to see how angry Godfrey was, especially considering his relationship with their father. Maybe, deep down, Godfrey held stronger feelings for their father than even he realized.

"But I won't," Godfrey added. "I want to see Gareth hang first."

"We promised you a pardon, and you will get one," Gwen added, "assuming you testify against Gareth. Will you?"

Firth nodded meekly, looking down, avoiding their gaze, still weeping.

"Of course you will," Godfrey added. "If you don't, we will kill you ourselves."

Godfrey dropped Firth, and he collapsed back down to the ground.

"I'm sorry," he said, over and over. "I'm sorry."

Gwen looked down at him, disgusted. She felt overwhelmed with sadness, thinking of her father, a noble, gallant man, having to die by this pathetic creature's hand. The dagger, still in her hand, positively shook, and she wanted to plunge it into Firth's heart herself.

But she did not. She wrapped it up carefully, and stuck in her waistband. She needed the evidence.

Now they had their witness.

And now it was time to bring down their brother.

CHAPTER TWENTY SEVEN

Thor stood at the helm of the ship, the sails full, the boat cruising beneath him, and his heart swelled as he saw, on the horizon, his homeland appearing. The Ring. It had been a long journey home, he and the Legion leaving the Isle of Mist in rough waters, fighting their way out to sea, then fighting their way through the rain wall. They had entered the open waters into a thick fog, and fog had enveloped them nearly the entire way home, luckily for them, allowing them to escape detection from the Empire the entire way back.

Now, with the Ring in sight, the two suns broke free, revealing a clear and perfect day. The wind caught, and the sails allowed them all a happy break from rowing. As Thor stood there, Krohn beside him, his bigger and stronger legs braced more sturdily on the wood, he stood taller, straighter, his shoulders broader, his jaw more full, and he stared with his narrow gray eyes at his homeland, his hair blowing in the wind.

In his palm he held the sparkling Orethist stone he'd salvaged from the dragon's shore. He could feel its power pulsing through him, and he smiled in anticipation as he imagined giving it to Gwen. He had been unable to shake her from this thoughts the entire ride home, and he realized now that she, more than anything else back home, was what mattered to him most, what he looked forward to most. He hoped that she still cared for him. Maybe she had moved on. After all, she was a Royal—she must have been introduced to hundreds of other boys in the meantime. He squeezed the jewel harder, closed his eyes, and silently prayed that she still cared for him even a fraction as much as he did for her.

He opened his eyes and on the horizon spotted the thick wood outlining the shores of the Ring. He breathed. It had been a long hundred days, the longest of his life, and he still could not believe he had survived it. He felt proud to be coming home, proud to have survived, and proud to be a true member of the Legion. He recalled the journey left to take through the woods, across the Canyon, back inside the energy shield of the Ring. He remembered how frightened he had been upon first leaving the Canyon, and marveled at how differently he felt now. He no longer held any fear. After his hundred days of grueling training, of every sort of combat, after facing the Cyclops and most of all, the Dragon, he realized that nothing scared him anymore. He was beginning to feel like a warrior.

Thor heard a familiar screeching noise, and looked up to see Ephistopheles. She was circling high above, following the ship. She swooped down and landed on the ship's rail, close by. She turned and screeched, looking right at Thor.

Thor was elated to see her, a reminder of home.

Just as quickly, she lifted into the air, flapping her wide wings. He knew he would see her again.

Thor reached down and lay a free hand on the hilt of his new sword. When they had finished the Hundred, before they had boarded the ships to return home, the Legion commanders had given each of the surviving boys a weapon, a token to symbolize that they were now full Legion members. Reese had been given a bejeweled shield; O'Connor, who walked now with a limp, still recovering from the dragon's blow, had been given a mahogany bow and arrow; Elden had been given a mace with a spiked silver ball—and Thor had been given this sword, its hilt wrapped with the finest silk, bejeweled, its blade sharper and smoother than any he had seen. Holding it in his hand, it felt like air.

As he squeezed its hilt tighter, he felt that he was now part of the Legion, a part of this band of brothers forever. They had gone through things together that no one else would ever understand. Thor looked over his brethren and could see that they looked older, too, stronger, toughened. They all looked like they had been through hell. And they had. He thought of all the brothers they had lost back there, boys they had started out with on this boat and who were not returning; boys who had dropped out along the way from cowardice; and boys who had been killed. It was sobering. Today was a cause for celebration—but it was also a cause for mourning. Not all of them had made it back. The weight of it was carried by all the Legion members, and Thor could detect a more serious, more mature look to them, the youthful giddiness they'd had just months ago gone, replaced with something else. A sense of mortality.

Thor would do anything now for these boys, his *real* brothers. And they all, since his rescuing them from the dragon, looked at him with a new respect.

Maybe, even, with a sense of awe. Even Kolk looked at him differently, with something like respect, and he had not reprimanded him once since.

Finally, Thor felt like he *belonged*. Whatever enemies he faced on shore no longer scared him. In fact, now, he welcomed combat.

Now, he understood what it meant to be a warrior.

*

Thor rode on horseback with the Legion, Reese on one side of him, O'Connor, Elden and the twins on the other, Krohn following below, all of them walking on the path towards King's court. He could hardly believe his eyes: before him, stretched as far as the eye could see, stood thousands of people, lining the road, screaming in adulation at their return. They waved banners, tossed candies at them, threw flower petals in their path. Military drums beat with precision, and cymbals and music rang out. It was the grandest parade that Thor had ever seen, and he rode at the center of it, surrounded by all his brothers

Thor had not expected a return welcome like this. Luckily, there journey back through the Canyon had been uneventful, and he had been shocked as they had crossed the bridge and the hundreds of King's soldiers had lowered their heads in deference to them. To *them*, boys. The guards had reached out and lowered their halberds, one at a time, in honor and respect. As Thor had walked through them, he had never felt more accepted, more of a sense of belonging, in his life. It made him feel that every minute of every hardship had been worth it. Here he was, respected by these great men, now a part of their ranks. There was nothing he had ever wanted more in life.

As they'd all set foot back on the safety of their side of the Canyon, they had been met with another surprise: there was a fleet of horses awaiting them, the most beautiful horses Thor had ever seen. Now, instead of having to tend the horses, to shovel their waste, Thor had been given one to ride himself. It was a thing of splendor, with a black hide and a long, white nose. He had named him Percival.

They had ridden for most of the day, cresting a small hill before reaching King's Court. When they'd reached its peak, Thor's breath had been taken away: as far as the eye could see, the masses lined King's Road, cheering them. The horizon was filled with Fall foliage and flowers, and it was a perfect day. They had left at Summer and returned at Fall, and the change was shocking.

As they all rode their horses now through the parade in King's Court, the sun beginning to set, Thor felt as if he were in a dream.

"Can you believe this is for us?" O'Connor asked, walking on his horse beside Thor.

"We're Legion members now," Elden said. "*Real* Legion members. If there's a war, we're called upon as reserves. We're not just trainees anymore: we're soldiers, too."

The masses cheered as they passed through, but as Thor looked over the faces, he was looking for only one person: Gwendolyn. It was all he thought of. Not riches or fame or honor, or any of it. He just wanted to see her, to know that she was still here, that she still cared for him.

The cheers reached a crescendo as the group reached King's Gate and crossed the wooden bridge, the bridge echoing beneath the weight of the horses' hooves. They continued on through the soaring arched stone, beneath the rows of iron spikes. They proceeded through the darkened part of the tunnel, then came out the other side, into King's Court.

As they did, they were met with a cheer, masses flooding the plaza from every direction, calling out their names. Thor was even amazed to hear some people call out his name—he could hardly believe that anyone even knew who he was.

As they continued into the plaza, Thor saw that banquet tables had been prepared for the festivities. He was beginning to realize that this day had been declared a holiday, and that all these festivities were just for them. It was hard to fathom.

They reached the center of the plaza, and standing there, waiting to greet them, was Brom, the lead general of all the armed forces. He was surrounded by his top generals, and by dozens of members of The Silver, and one by one, the boys dismounted and walked towards them, stopping at attention as they lined up.

Kolk walked around and stood beside Brom, and the two of them stood side by side, facing the boys. The crowd fell silent.

"Men," Brom called out, "for from now on you shall be called *men*—we welcome you home as members of the Legion!"

The crowd cheered, and knights of The Silver stepped forward and pinned each boy with a pin, a black falcon holding a sword, the emblem of the Legion, on their left breast, above their hearts. Each Legion member was pinned by the knight he was squire to—and Thor was upset that Erec and Kendrick were both not there to pin him. Kolk, in their place, stepped forward and pinned him. He looked down and, to Thor's surprise, slowly broke into a smile.

"You're not half bad," he said.

It was the first time Thor had ever seen him smile. Then Kolk quickly frowned and hurried off.

The masses cheered, and musicians started up, drums and lutes and cymbals and harps, and the crowd broke into celebration.

Casks of ale were rolled out onto the fields, and a foaming glass of ale was soon shoved into Thor's hand. Within moments, it became an all-out party.

Someone came up behind Thor and lifted him up onto his shoulders, and Thor found himself hoisted in the air, along with this brethren, holding his glass of ale as it spilled, laughing as he was jostled in the air. Thor reached over and clinked glasses with Reese, also on a stranger's shoulders, off-balance, laughing. He swayed and eventually fell off, landing on his feet with the others.

Songs and dancing broke out everywhere, and Thor found himself locking arms with some woman he did not recognize, a stranger who grabbed his arm and danced with him in circles, spinning him around and around, in one direction, then the other. Thor, caught off guard, finally broke away; he did not want to dance with her. Although all the other Legion members were dancing with random strangers, Thor did not want to be with anyone else. He only wanted Gwendolyn.

He searched for her frantically through the crowd. Had she come? Was she still interested in him?

The crowd grew rowdier, and the sun began to set, torches were lit and the drink grew stronger. Jugglers appeared, throwing flaming sticks, sporting events ensued, and huge spits of meat were rolled out. Thor was thrilled to be in the middle of it—but without seeing Gwendolyn, something was missing.

"Hey, that's my girl!" someone screamed threateningly.

Thor turned and saw O'Connor, with his limp, dancing with a girl, then saw a drunken stranger approach and shove O'Connor hard. The man was tall and beefy, and O'Connor stumbled back several feet, caught off guard.

The bully continued towards O'Connor, but before he could take another foot, Thor, reacting instinctively, jumped into action—as did the other Legion members around him. Within seconds, Thor, Reese, Elden and the twins pounced on the man, knocking him down to the ground.

The man scurried up, fear in his eyes, and ran off.

Thor turned back to O'Connor, who was fine, but dazed. As Thor looked over at his brothers, he realized how quickly they had come to each other's defense, realized that they were now all truly one unit, there for each other. It felt good.

Thor saw all the people dancing, and his thoughts returned to Gwendolyn. He searched for her everywhere, breaking away from the dancing area, leaving his brethren, and walking up and down the rows of banquet tables. He had to find her.

He jumped up on a bench, trying to peer above the crowd. But he saw no sight of her, and his heart fell.

He jumped down and saw an attendant from the castle, a girl he recognized, a beautiful girl, maybe seventeen, and ran up to her. She turned to look at him, and her eyes lit up in adulation. She was flirting with him.

"Thorgrin!" she exclaimed.

She embraced him, and he gently pushed her away.

"Have you seen Gwendolyn?" he asked.

She shook her head, and looked into his eyes.

"I have not," she said. "But I am here. Would you like to dance with me?"

Thor gently shook his head and hurried off, not wanting to get embroiled with anyone else.

He looked everywhere for Gwen, on all corners of the field, and was starting to think the worst. Maybe she had run off with someone else. Maybe her mother had gotten to her, had forbidden their relationship. Maybe she didn't feel the same way about him.

Suddenly, Thor felt a tap on his shoulder.

He spun, and his world melted.

Standing there, just a few feet away, smiling back, was the love of his life.

Gwendolyn.

*

Thor was mesmerized. Gwendolyn looked as beautiful as ever, staring back with her wide smile, her perfect skin, her long, blonde hair, her large blue eyes. It was like meeting her for the first time. He could look nowhere else, his heart pounded. He felt as if he had truly returned.

Gwendolyn jumped into his arms, embracing him tightly, and he embraced her back. He could hardly believe that someone like her could love him, and he loved her back with everything he had. He hugged her for a very long time, and she did not let go.

"I'm so glad you're back," she whispered earnestly into his ear.

"As am I," he answered.

He felt her hot tears running down his neck, and slowly, he pulled back. He leaned in and kissed her, and they held the kiss for a long time, as people jostled them in every direction, shouts and cheers all around them as the crowd swirled.

There came a whining, and Gwen looked down in delight to see Krohn, jumping up on her, whining. She reached down and petted him, kissing him and laughing as he jumped on her and licked her face.

"I missed you," she said.

Krohn whined.

Gwen stood, smiling, and looked back to Thor, the last rays of sunset lit up her eyes, and she reached out and took his hand.

"Come with me," she said.

He did not need prodding. She lead him through the crowd, zigzagging this way and that, Krohn following, until finally she lead him through an ancient gate, and into the royal gardens.

They were back in the labyrinth of formal gardens, and it was quiet here, the cheers of the masses muted. They had privacy, finally, and they held hands as she faced him.

They kissed again, for a long time.

Finally she pulled back.

"Not a day passed that I did not think of you," Thor said to her.

She smiled.

"And I you," she said, looking into his eyes. "I prayed every day for your safe return."

Thor smiled as he reached into his pocket, and slowly pulled out the stone he had been dying to give her.

"Close your eyes," he said, "and open your hand."

She closed her eyes, smiled, and tentatively held out a palm.

"It's not a snake, is it?" she asked.

He laughed.

"No, I think not," he said.

Thor reached out and gingerly place into her palm the piece of Orethist he had found on Dragon's isle.

Gwen opened her eyes, and examined it in wonder.

The stone lay in her palm, glowing like a living thing, attached to the silver necklace chain Thor had forged.

"It's beautiful!" she exclaimed.

"It is Orethist. A rock from the shore of Dragon's isle. It is said to have magical powers. Legend has it that, if you give it to someone you love, it will save their life."

Gwen looked down and blushed as he said the word "love."

"You brought this all the way back for me?" she asked.

She looked at it in awe as Thor took the necklace, came around behind her, and fastened it on her neck. She reached down and felt it, then turned and hugged Thor tight.

"Is the most beautiful thing I've ever been given," she said. "I will cherish it forever."

She took his hand and led him deeper into the twisting and turning pathways of the gardens.

"I'm afraid I have nothing to give you in return," she said.

"You've given me everything," he said. "You're still here."

She smiled, clutching his hand.

"We can be together now," she said. "My mother...she's not in her right mind. I'm sorry for her. But happy for us. We have no more obstacles between us."

"I have to admit, I was afraid that when I returned, you might be with someone else," he said.

"How could you think such a thing?" she scolded.

Thor shrugged, embarrassed.

"I don't know. You have so many others to choose from."

She shook her head.

"You don't understand. I've already chosen. I want to be with you forever."

He stopped and turned and kissed her, a kiss that lasted forever under the fading light of twilight. At her words, Thor was happier than he'd ever been. Because that was exactly what he wanted, too.

She looked embarrassed.

"And I have to admit something, too," she said.

Thor looked at her, puzzled.

"I was afraid you might not think me beautiful anymore," she said, eyes lowered, "because of my scar."

"What scar?" Thor asked.

"Here, on this cheek," she said, pointing to the scratch that Gareth's dog had left.

Thor squinted at it, puzzled.

"I can't even see it," he said.

"That's because it is nearly dark. In the light of day it is more visible."

He shook his head.

"You imagine it to be greater than it is," he said. "It is but a trace. Inches away, I can barely see it. And besides, it does not detract from your beauty— if anything, it adds to it."

She felt her heart warming, felt reassured, realizing he was genuine, and leaned in and kissed him.

"I was attacked," she said as she pulled back.

Thor's face darkened, and he lowered his hand instinctively to the hilt of his sword.

"By who?" he demanded. "Tell me who it was, and I will kill him right now."

She shook her head.

"That does not matter now," she said, her face darkening. "He's already dead. What matters now is that you should know that there are big changes about to happen here," she said. "King's Court will never be the same."

"What do you mean?" he asked, concerned. "Is everything okay?"

She slowly shook her head.

"It is and it's not. My brother, Kendrick, has been imprisoned."

"What!?" Thor cried, outraged.

"Gareth has set him up, accused him of murdering my father. All lies. My father's murderer—we have discovered him. Finally, we have proof."

Thor's eyes opened wide.

"It was Gareth," she said.

Thor felt his body go cold with the news. He hardly knew what to say. He tried to think of what that meant for the King's Army, the Legion, for the kingdom, for Kendrick—it was too much to process. He hated to think that he was swearing allegiance to a king who was a murderer.

"What will you do?" he asked her.

"We have a witness to the crime. Tomorrow, my brother Godfrey and I, we will confront Gareth. We will bring him to justice. And King's Court will be without a king."

Thor tried to process all of this. His mind spun with the implications. He was happy that MacGil's murderer had finally been found, yet he was worried for Gwen's safety.

"Does that mean you will free Kendrick tomorrow?"

"Yes," she said. "Tomorrow, everything will change. We only found our witness hours ago, and we were awaiting your return. We wanted the Legion to be here, to back us up when we confront Gareth, in case there is a revolt. He will not go down easily."

Thor breathed.

"I will do whatever I can, my lady, to make sure justice is done for your father. And to keep you safe."

She leaned in and kissed him, and he kissed her back. A fall breeze caressed them, and he never wanted this night to end.

"I love you," she said.

He felt a thrill at her words. It was the first time she had said it—the first time that any girl had ever said those words to him.

He looked into her eyes, a glistening blue, lit up in the twilight, and in them, he saw his own reflection. It was a face he almost did not recognize. Every day, he felt as if he were becoming someone new.

"I love you, too," he said back.

They kissed again, and for the first time in as long as he could remember, everything felt right in the world.

CHAPTER TWENTY EIGHT

King McCloud could hardly believe his good luck, how deep his men were penetrating into MacGil territory. It had been over three months, an entire season, of rape and pillage and murder, leaving a trail of destruction from East to West as they tore into the heart of the Western Kingdom of the Ring. It had been a hundred straight days—more than any he had spent in his life—filled with glory, victory. He was sated with wine, and cattle, and spoils, and heads, and women. He could not get enough.

McCloud closed his eyes as he galloped farther and farther West, into the setting of the second sun, and he smiled as in his mind flashed the faces of all the men he had murdered. There were the innocent villagers, caught off guard, trying to put up their pitiful defenses; there were the professional soldiers of the King's guard, horribly outmanned, underequipped and unprepared. Those kills were the most enjoyable—at least they had put up something of a fight. Though they never stood a chance: McCloud's men were too motivated, too disciplined. They knew that every battle they fought was to the death. Because if they lost, or did not fight hard enough, McCloud would have his own men killed. He had trained his soldiers well.

The McCloud army had been a killing machine as they went from town to town, claiming territory, making it their own. Like a violent storm of locusts passing through the land, nothing had been able to stop them.

McCloud had also made it a priority to surround each village first, block all the exits, and prevent the escape of any messengers that might escape to King's Court and alert the greater MacGil army of the invasion. He had managed to murder them all, to keep this invasion a secret for so long. He hoped to surprise MacGil's army, and wipe them all out before they had time to muster a defense. Then he could march into King's Court, make Gareth surrender, and claim the entire Ring as his own.

They galloped, McCloud's entourage having grown larger with all the slaves he had captured, all the boys and old men he had forced to join his troop. He now charged with at least a thousand men, hardened warriors all of them, a huge killing machine. In the distance he could already see the next town, its steeples visible even from here. This town, he could see, was larger than most, a small city, a sure sign that they were getting closer to King's Court.

As they neared it, McCloud could tell from the walls that this was the last major city before the direct approach to King's Court. They were still a good three days ride away, far enough away that the MacGils could not reinforce them quickly. They stood no chance against McCloud's Army.

They galloped harder. The sound of horses' hooves rose in his ears, the dust rose off the road, filling his nostrils, and he could see townsmen scurrying to close the gate, lowering the huge iron bars. McCloud was almost impressed. Most of the other towns had no stone walls, no iron gates—just a lame set of parameters. This town was larger, more sophisticated, prepared for a siege.

But as McCloud studied its walls with his professional soldier's eye, he saw that, most importantly, it was devoid of soldiers. It was guarded by just a handful of boys and elder men, posted at stations spread too far among the wall. The holes were plentiful. McCloud could tell that they would overrun it within minutes.

They might try to surrender, as others had. But he would not give them that chance. That would take away half the fun.

"Charge!" he screamed.

Behind him, his men screamed in approval, and together, they sprinted for the town, McCloud riding out front as he always did. As they got close to the city gate, McCloud reached down, yanked a huge spear off the horse's harness, and chucked it.

It was a perfect strike, planting in the back of the boy who had been running across the courtyard, trying to close the gate. He had succeeded in closing the gate—but that would be the final success of his young life.

That iron gate could not keep them out. As they rode up to it, McCloud's men, well-trained, pulled their horses up before it, while others dismounted, jumped on top of their fellow's horse, and allowed themselves to be picked up and thrown over the wall. One at a time, McCloud's men landed on the other side, and then finally unlocked the gate for the rest of them.

His army charged through, a thousand men strong, poring through the small opening.

McCloud was the first to gallop through, determined to be the first to wreak bloodshed. He drew his sword and chased down men and women as they ran. How many men, in how many towns, he mused, would run from him like this? It was the same scene in every place he visited. Nothing in the Ring could stop him now.

By rote, McCloud grabbed a small throwing axe from his waist, leaned back, took aim at the center of a man's back he decided he did not like, and let it fly. It tumbled end over end, and impaled the man with a satisfying noise, like a spear entering a tree.

The man shrieked and fell flat on his face, and McCloud had his horse trampled over him, making sure he ran over his head. McCloud felt a thrill of satisfaction as the horse ran over him. He would come back for his axe later.

McCloud singled out a particularly young and beautiful woman, perhaps twenty, as she ran for her house. He kicked his horse at a full gallop and bore down on her. As they pulled up alongside her he jumped off and landed on top of her, tackling her down to the ground, her soft body and large bosom cushioning his fall.

She screamed and cried out, dazed from the attack, as they rolled on the ground. He backhanded her, silencing her.

He then lifted her over his shoulder as he got to his feet, and made his way towards the first empty dwelling he could find. He smiled as his army galloped past, as he heard the screams, saw the bloodshed all around him. This would be a wonderful night.

*

Luanda wept as she rode on the back of Bronson's horse into the walled town of her homeland, the town of her sister's mother, and watched the McClouds ravage it, as they had so many towns along the way. She'd had no choice but to ride along with them, all these days, and she had learned to keep her mouth shut, had been disciplined one too many times by the elder McCloud. She had done her best to keep quiet, to try to fit in as a McCloud, to justify to herself the attacking and pillaging of her homeland. But finally, she could stand it no longer: something inside her head snapped. She recognized this town, which she had spent time in as a child. It was but a few days' ride from King's Court, and the sight of it made her knees weak and brought a well of emotion. Finally, she'd had enough.

She had felt defenseless in the face of the strength of a foreign army, but now, so close to home, she felt in her home territory, and felt a new surge of strength. She felt a renewed sense that she had to stop this. She could not let things go on like this. In but a few days they would reach King's Court, and who knew what damage these savages would do to her hometown when she got there.

She had fallen in love with Bronson, despite everything, who was nothing like his father and who, in fact, despised him, too; but marrying into this McCloud clan, she had realized, had been a mistake. They were nothing like her people. They all cowered under the iron fist of the elder McCloud.

At least her husband had not partaken in the savagery, as had the others. He put on a good show of it for his father, but she knew him well, already. As he entered this new town, he rode off to the side and made himself scarce, while the others did the damage. He dismounted and fidgeted with his horse, pretending it was hurt, trying to appear busy while he did his best not to hurt anyone.

He helped Luanda dismount, as he always did, and she sobbed and rushed into his arms, squeezing him hard.

"Make it stop!" she screamed into his ear.

He held her tight, and she could feel his love for her.

"I'm sorry, my love," he said. "I wish I could."

"Sorry is not good enough," she yelled, pulling back and staring to his eyes, summoning all the fierceness of her own father. After all, she, too, came from a long line of kings. "You are killing my people!"

"I am not," he said, looking down. "My father is."

"You and your father are of the same family! The same dynasty. You go along with it."

He looked up, skittish.

"You know my father. How am I supposed to stop him? This army? I can't control him," he said with remorse.

She could see in his eyes how much he wanted to—but how powerless he was in the face of him.

"Anyone can be stopped," she said. "No one is that powerful. Look at him, there he goes now," she said, turning and pointing, watching, disgusted, as the elder McCloud carried off on another young, innocent, unconscious girl to be his play thing for the night.

"Your father will be defenseless in there," she said. "I don't need you. I can sneak up on him myself and while he is sleeping, strike a peg through his skull."

Emboldened by her own idea, she reached into the horse's harness and extracted a long, sharp spike. Without thinking, she turned to go, determined to do exactly that—to kill the elder McCloud on her own.

But as she went, a strong hand grabbed her arm and held her in place.

She wheeled and saw Bronson staring back.

"You don't know my father," he said. "He is invincible. He carries the strength of ten men. And he is more wily than a rat. He will sense your approach a mile away. He will strip you of your weapon and kill you, before you even get through the door. That is not the way," he said. "There are other ways."

She looked at him closely, examining him, wondering what he was saying.

"Are you saying that you will help me?"

"I hate my father as much as you do," he said. "I can't stop his army while it advances. But if his army fails, I am prepared to take action."

He stared back at her, meaningfully, and she could tell that he was earnest—but she also could not tell if he had the resolve to carry through. He was a good man. But when it came to his father, he was weak.

She shook her head.

"That's not good enough," she said. "My people are dying now. They can't wait. And neither can I. I will kill him now, by myself. And if I fail—at least I will die trying."

With those words, Luanda threw his hand off of her and turned and marched for the tent, holding the iron spike, shaking with fear, but determined to kill this monster once and for all.

CHAPTER TWENTY NINE

Gwendolyn walked quickly, side by side with Thor in the early morning, twisting and turning their way down the castle corridors, Krohn following. They walked with purpose, heading towards the council chamber, and Gwen took a deep breath, stealing herself for her confrontation with Gareth. The time of reckoning had come, and while nervous, she also felt a great sense of relief. Finally, after all these months, she had the proof she needed to bring her father's murderer to justice.

She had planned with Godfrey to meet him outside the chamber, with Firth, so that they could all three march in and confront Gareth at this meeting—in front of all the councilmembers—and to publicly prove his guilt. Thor had offered to accompany her, and it was an offer she accepted gladly. After last night, a long, magical night together, she did not want to part from his side, and she felt more secure having him there as backup. Of course the chamber would be filled with councilmembers and guards who would have no choice but to back her up and arrest Gareth once the proof came to light. But having Thor there gave her an extra layer of assurance.

They turned another corner, and Gwen smiled to herself as she thought of her night with Thor. She had slept in his arms amidst the flowers, in the royal gardens, the fall breezes caressing them all night long. They had fallen asleep looking up at the stars, and it had been divine. Her life had been upside down since the death of her father, in a constant state of anxiety and turmoil, but now, with Thor's return, and with Gareth about to be deposed and Kendrick about to be freed, she felt that things would finally return to a semblance of normal.

As they marched down the final, long corridor that led to the Council chamber, her heart was pounding. She could not underestimate Gareth, and she knew he would not take this well. He had lived his whole life to rule, and he would do anything he could to keep power, to hold onto his throne. He could be a very convincing liar, and she tried to prepare herself for his denials, his recriminations. She just prayed that Firth would be consistent, would be a strong witness against him. She assumed that his testimony, along with the presentation of the murder weapon, which she kept in her waist, would leave no room for doubt.

"You okay?" Thor asked sweetly, reaching over and taking her hand. He must have sensed her nervousness.

Gwen nodded back, squeezing his hand, then letting go.

The two of them continued down the corridor, their footsteps echoing, passing rows of open-aired windows, the early morning light streaking in. She felt what it would be like to march somewhere with Thor by her side. As a couple. It felt good. Natural. She felt a sense of peace in his presence. She felt stronger.

They reached the end of the corridor, and turned and faced the huge, arched oak doors to the council room. She heard muffled voices behind it, and before it stood several guards.

As she stood there, Gwen was confused. Godfrey and Firth were supposed to be waiting for her here, to meet her and walk in together. She had gone over the plan with Godfrey several times—she could not understand where he was. They had both been precise about it. Without them there, how could she proceed?

"My lady?" a guard asked. "I'm afraid a Council session is in progress."

"Has my brother been here? Godfrey?" she asked.

The guards looked at each other, puzzled.

"No, my lady."

Gwen's heart pounded. Something was wrong. Godfrey wouldn't not show up. Where could he be? Had he reverted to his ways, had he gone back to the taverns? Was he drinking? And where was Firth? She sensed deep down that something was wrong. Very, very wrong.

She stood there, torn, and debated what to do. She couldn't walk away. Not now. There was too much at stake, and no time left to lose. If she had to do this on her own, then she would.

She was about to command the guards to let her in, when suddenly there came a great rumble of footsteps from down the opposite corridor. She and Thor spun, and saw approaching them a contingent of a dozen soldiers, Brom leading the pack. He wore a deep scowl and a look of grave concern, and he marched quickly, the others on his tail, all members of The Silver, famous warriors each.

"Open these doors at once," Brom commanded the guards.

"But sire, a Council meeting is in session," said one of the guards tentatively, looking very nervous.

Brom quickly moved one hand to his hilt, menacing.

"I'm not going to tell you again," he growled.

The guards exchanged a glance, then quickly stepped aside and yanked open the doors.

Brom, furious, marched right past them, into the Council chamber, followed by his men.

Gwen and Thor exchanged a puzzled look, then followed them in.

Gwen was baffled; this was not going as she had planned. She had to find out what was going on, and to decide if now was the right time to confront Gareth.

As they followed them in, the big doors slammed closed behind them, and a dozen councilmembers, seated in a broad semi-circle, in ancient, oak chairs, all turned. Gareth sat in the center of the room, on his throne, and looked up, surprised. Gareth scowled.

"Well, well," Gareth said. "If it isn't Brom. If I recall, you quit this council."

"I have come to deliver dire news," Brom said hastily. "Our men tell us of a breach of the Highlands. A full scale invasion of the McClouds. Entire villages wiped out. It seems the McClouds have found their opportunity in your reign. They are murdering our people even as we speak. War has begun."

Gwen felt the wind taken from her; she could hardly believe this news, as she stood several feet behind them, watching the whole thing. She watched Gareth's face transform, to one of shock. He sat there, frozen, not responding.

"What do you propose we do?" Brom prodded.

"What do you mean?" Gareth asked, nervous.

"I mean, what is your command? What is your strategy? How do you plan to meet their forces? Which formations will you choose? Which armies will you send out? Which will stay at home? And what will be our counterattack? How many fortifications will be manned? And how do you propose we defend the villages?"

Gareth sat there, opening his mouth to speak several times, then closing it. He looked stumped, flustered, clearly in way over his head.

"I…" he began, clearing his throat, then stopped. "I think…maybe it's not as bad as you think. Let's wait and see what happens."

"Wait and see what happens?" Brom echoed, aghast.

"We can always deal with it later, if they get too close," Gareth said. "It's probably just a raid, and they'll go back home soon. Besides, we have a festival coming up, and I don't want the preparations for our parties disturbed."

Brom stared back at him with a look of shock and disgust. Finally, his face turned a shade of purple.

"You are a disgrace to your father's memory," Brom said.

With that, Brom turned and stormed from the room, his men following.

Gareth rose and bunched his fists, red-faced.

"You get back here!" Gareth screamed. "Don't you ever turn your back on your King! That is treason. I will have you arrested! You will do as I command! Brom! BROM! ARREST HIM!"

But the guards stood there, frozen, afraid to go near Brom.

Brom stormed out of the chamber, his men following, and Gwen and Thor turned and hurried out after them.

Back out in the open hall, the doors slammed behind them, Gwen hurried over to Brom as he began to march off.

"Sire!" she yelled.

Brom stopped and turned, still heated.

"My lady," he said with deference, but impatience. "Your father would have never accepted that," he added, still fuming.

"I know," she answered. "My father never would have accepted many things happening here. What do you plan to do? About the invasion?"

"I must act. What other choice do I have? I can't sit by and watch my homeland destroyed. I will act with or without the authority of the King. I will mobilize our forces on my own. I will take control of the army. It is heresy, but I have no choice. We must defend."

"That is exactly what you should do," she said.

He looked at her, and seemed to calm momentarily.

"I am glad to hear a member of the royal family say that," he said. "It is unfortunate that you are not the one on the throne."

"There is another member of the royal family you should care about," she said. "My brother Kendrick sits wallowing in the dungeon. He would be a key asset to your forces. The men love him, and would rally around him. And as a royal family member, he would give you the authority and them the confidence they need to attack."

He studied her, looking impressed.

"But Kendrick has been imprisoned for murder. For treason."

Gwen shook her head.

"Lies. All of them. He is innocent. In fact, I have found proof absolving Kendrick of guilt. He was setup by the real murderer."

Brom looked back at her, wide-eyed.

"And who then is the murderer?" he asked.

"Gareth," she answered.

Brom's eyes opened wide in wonder. Finally, he nodded back knowingly.

"We will take care of Gareth when we return from battle," he said. "In the meantime, you are correct. We will free Kendrick, and he will help lead us in battle. To the dungeons!"

The group of them turned and hurried down the twisting corridors of the castle, their footsteps echoing like thunder. They descended down the spiral staircase, flight after flight, spiraling all the way down, until they reached the lowest level.

265

Several guards blocked an iron cell door, and they stiffened at attention at the sight of Brom and all The Silver.

"Open this door at once!" Brom commanded.

"My liege," the guard said, shakily. "I'm afraid I can only open this on royal command."

"I am commander of the seven legions of the Western kingdom of the Ring!" Brom threatened, resting a hand on his hilt. "I say open this door at once!"

The guards stood there, vacillating, looking at each other, nervous.

Gwen could see a confrontation was about to happen, so she stepped forward in the tense silence and stood between them.

"I am of the royal family," she said calmly. "My father, bless his memory, was King not long ago. I act with his authority. Open this door."

The guards looked at each other, then nodded, and slowly reached out and unlocked the door.

Brom and his group marched down to the very end of the corridor and stopped in front of Kendrick's cell.

Kendrick rushed to it, and pressed his face against the bars, looking pale and gaunt. Gwen felt heartbroken to see him like this, and that she had not been able to free him sooner.

"Open this door," Gwen commanded the guard, who had accompanied them.

The guard stepped forward and unlocked the cell. The door opened slowly, and out came Kendrick.

Kendrick gave Gwendolyn a big hug, and she hugged him back, tightly.

Kendrick turned and looked at Brom. He saluted, and Brom saluted back.

"The McClouds have attacked," Brom said. "You will lead one of our forces in battle. We must go at once."

Kendrick nodded back, somber.

"Sire, it will be an honor."

"Do you wish to have your squire back?" Thor asked, with a smile.

Kendrick turned and looked at Thor, and his face lit up with a smile.

"I have just returned from the Hundred, sire," Thor said, "I am ready. And it would be an honor to ride by your side."

Kendrick reached out and laid a hand on Thor's shoulder. He looked him up and down, and nodded approvingly.

"I can see that you are. I would have no one else by my side."

"Let's move," Brom said. "It's past time we teach these McClouds what it means to invade our side of the Ring."

The group turned and began marching back down the hall.

Soon they were upstairs and marching out the main front doors of the castle. As they exited, standing on Castle Bridge, Thor stopped and faced Gwen.

He looked at her with a look of concern and longing.

"I must join my brothers," he said guiltily. "I hate to leave you. But I must defend our Ring."

Deep down, her heart was breaking, but she did not show it. She nodded back.

"I know," she said, trying to sound strong. "You must go."

Selfishly she wanted him to stay, but she knew that his going was the right thing.

Thor reached out and touched her necklace, then reached up with the back of his hand and stroked her face. He leaned in and kissed her, and she held it as long as she could.

"I will think of you every minute," Thor said. "I will return as soon as I can. And when I do, I want to ask you a question."

Gwen smiled, puzzled.

"What question?"

Thor smiled back.

"It is one, I think, that will change our lives. Depending, of course, on your answer."

He grabbed her hand, pulled it up and kissed her fingertips, then turned with a smile, and trotted off to join the other men, Krohn following, already running for their horses.

Gwen watched him go with a sense of longing and admiration. She prayed with all she had that she would see him again.

CHAPTER THIRTY

Erec galloped through the back streets of Savaria, racing to the tavern. He was eager to pick up Alistair, to rescue her from this place and to ride off with her. He was exhausted from the day's battle, covered in bruises and cuts, weak from hunger and thirst—but still, he could think of nothing but her. He could not stop, could not rest, until he had her with him.

Dressed in his chain mail, Erec pulled up before the tavern, jumped off his horse and hurried through the door. It burst open and he walked in expecting to see Alistair there, waiting for him.

But he was baffled to see that she was not. Instead, he saw only the bartender, surly, standing behind the bar. Ten large, seedy types sat at the bar before him.

Erec looked everywhere, but saw no sign of her. The patrons grew quiet, however, and the room grew thick with tension. Erec did not understand what was going on.

The bartender nodded to an attendant, who turned and ran through the door to the back room. A moment later, the innkeeper exited, waltzing out with a swagger, and a crooked smile on his face. Erec did not like the look of this.

"Where is my bride?" he demanded, stepping forward.

The innkeeper strutted out towards him.

"Well well well, look who it is," he said.

As he marched towards him, Erec noticed several of the burly miscreants get up and follow in behind him.

"If it isn't the knight in shining armor himself," the innkeeper mocked.

"I'm not going to ask you again," Erec said. "Where is she?" he pressed, his anger rising.

The innkeeper's smile broadened.

"Well, it's funny you should ask. You see, the large sum of money you handed me gave me an idea. I figured if Alistair was worth something to you, maybe she was worth something to somebody else, too. And I was right. Probably one of the better business deals I've made," he said, licking his lips and laughing, as the men laughed around him.

Erec was seething, turning a shade of purple.

Through clenched teeth, he growled: "This is your last chance. Where—is—she?"

The innkeeper smiled, reveling in the moment.

"Well, it seems she was worth even more to someone else than she was to you. I sold her to a slave trader, willing to buy her for five hundred pence. He had been coming through town, looking for some whores to add to his sex trade. Sorry. You're too late. But thanks for the idea. And I'll be keeping your sack of gold anyway, as compensation for insulting my friends the other night."

The innkeeper stood there, grinning, hands on his hips.

"Now you can be on your way," he added, "before we all do you more harm than you wish."

As Erec studied this miscreant's self-satisfied eyes, he could unfortunately see that everything he was saying was true. He could not believe it. His Alistair. Taken away from him. Sold into slavery, into the sex trade. And all of this because of this disgusting human being before him.

Erec could stand it no longer. He was overwhelmed with an urge not only to fight, but for vengeance.

The innkeeper's men lunged at Erec, and Erec wasted no time. He had been trained to fight with multiple men, on multiple occasions, and was used to situations like this. These men had no idea who they were attacking.

As a huge man grabbed him, Erec tucked himself into a role, grabbing his arm, and throwing him over his shoulder. Without hesitating, Erec spun around and back-kicked another in the groin, wheeled around and elbowed one in the face, then leaned forward and head-butted the fourth, the bartender. The four of them fell to the floor.

Erec heard the distinct sound of a sword being drawn, and looked over to see three more miscreants coming at him, swords drawn.

He didn't waste any time: he reached down and extracted a dagger from his waist, and as the first man lunged at him with his sword, he plunged into his throat. The man screamed out, gurgling blood, and Erec reached over and grabbed the sword from his hand. He spun around, chopped off one man's head, then turned and plunged the sword into the heart of the third.

The three men fell, dead.

Seven men on the ground, not moving, and the innkeeper, the last one left, looked at Erec now with fear.

He stumbled back two steps, realizing he had made a big mistake—but it was too late. Erec charged, jumped into the air, and kicked him so hard he went flying back, over the tables, crashing to the ground.

Erec took a wooden bench, lifted it high, and shattered it into pieces over the man's head. The innkeeper collapsed, blood coming from his head, and Erec landed on top of him.

The man tried to pull a dagger from his waist, but Erec saw it coming and stepped on his wrist until he screamed, then kicking the dagger away with his other foot.

Erec leaned down and choked him. The man gurgled.

"Where is she?" Erec demanded. "Where exactly was the slave trader going?"

"I will never tell you," the man gasped.

Erec squeezed harder, until he turned a shade of purple. He took his dagger, held it between the man's legs, and began to press harder and harder, until the innkeeper screamed, a high-pitched noise.

"Last chance," Erec warned. He pushed even harder, and the man screeched, and finally yelled out.

"Okay! The man was heading south, on the Southern Lane. He was heading towards Baluster. He left early yesterday morning. That's all I know. I swear!"

Erec scowled down at him, satisfied he had told the truth, and pulled back the dagger.

Then, in one quick motion, he thrust it into his heart.

The innkeeper sat up, eyes bulging wide, gasping for air, and Erec turned the dagger deeper and deeper, pulling the man close, and looking into his eyes as he died.

"That is for Alistair."

CHAPTER THIRTY ONE

Gwen had no time to lose. She had to see if Godfrey and Firth were waiting for her now, outside the Council chamber, to confront Gareth. Perhaps they had been delayed, and were standing there. She could not let them go in alone. They had to make their case now, while the Council was still in session. If Kendrick and Thor and Brom and all the others could risk their lives in battle for their homeland, the least she could do is take an example of their bravery and risk her safety on the home front to stop Gareth. After all, if a new ruler was crowned, it would help the army greatly. Including Thor.

Gwen ran up the steps then down the castle corridor, until she reached the huge doors to the chamber. To her dismay, Godfrey and Firth were still not there. She had no idea what could have happened to them. The doors to the Council chamber were open, and as she glanced inside, she saw that the Council had already left, the session ended. The only person who remained in the vast, empty chamber was Gareth. He sat there, alone on his throne in the cavernous room, rubbing its arms.

It was just the two of them now, and Gwen decided that now was the time. Maybe being alone, she could pound sense into him and get him to step down quietly. The men she loved were out there in battle, fighting for her and all the others, and she felt she had to fight, too. She could not wait. She would confront him with what she knew, and hopefully, he would voluntarily step down. She didn't care if he went quietly, without fanfare; she just wanted him out.

Gwen walked through the doors, her footsteps echoing as she entered the huge chamber, as she walked towards her brother, in the ancient, enormous room, light pouring in through the stained-glass windows behind him. Gareth looked up at her with cold, soulless black eyes, and she could feel the hatred he held for her. She could see in that paranoid stare of his what a threat she was to him. Perhaps it was because their father loved her more. Or perhaps he was just born to hate.

"I wish to have a word with you," Gwen announced, her voice too loud, echoing in this place of politics which she hated. It was eerie, seeing her brother seated there on her father's throne. She did not like the feeling. It felt wrong. His eyes were hollow, and he looked like he had aged a hundred years. He looked nothing like their father did on that throne. Her father had sat on it naturally, looking noble, gallant, proud, looking as if the throne were meant for him. Gareth sat on it in a way that seemed desperate, overreaching, as if he were sitting in a seat too big for him to fill. Maybe she was picking up her dead father's feelings, pouring through her. A fury rose within her over what Gareth had done to her father. He had taken him away from her.

At the same time, she was afraid. She knew how vindictive Gareth could be, and knew this would not go well.

Gareth stared back wordlessly. She waited, but he said nothing.

Finally she cleared her throat, her heart pounding, and continued.

"I know that you had father killed," she said, wanting to get it over with. "I know that Firth did the stabbing. We have the murder weapon. We have the dagger."

There was a long silence, and Gareth, to his credit, remained expressionless the entire time.

Finally, he let out a short, derisive snort.

"You are a foolish, fanciful, young girl," he said. "You always have been. No one believes you. No one ever will. You envy me because I sit on the throne instead of you. That is your sole motivation. You speak nonsense."

"Do I?" she asked.

"You put father up to naming you heir instead of me," Gareth countered. "You manipulated him in your greed for power. I saw through you ever since you were a child. But it did not work. I am here. And you cannot stand it."

Gwen shook her head, amazed at how pathetic Gareth was. He projected his own feelings onto everybody else. He was pathological. She shuddered to think she was related to him.

"The people will decide how fanciful I am," she said. "Did I imagine this weapon in my hand?" she asked, reaching into her waist and extracting the dagger. She held it out for him to see, and his eyes opened wide for the first time.

For the first time, he sat upright, gripping the sides of the throne.

"Where did you get that?" he asked.

Finally, he was caught. She could see it in his face, clear as day. She still could hardly believe it. He had killed their father.

"You disgust me," she said. "You are a pathetic human being. I wish father were here to take his vengeance himself. But he is not. So I will seek justice in his stead. You will be tried and convicted and you will be killed. And our father's soul will be laid to rest."

"And how will you do that, exactly?" he asked. "Do you really think the masses will believe you because you found a blood-stained dagger? Anyone could have wielded it. Where is your proof?"

"I have a witness," she said. "The man who wielded the weapon."

To her surprise, Gareth smiled.

"Do you mean Firth?" he asked. "Don't worry: we won't be hearing much from him."

Now it was Gwendolyn's turn to be caught off guard; her heart pounded at the ominous tone of his words.

"What do you mean?" she asked, unsure.

"Firth is long gone from us, I'm afraid. It is so unfortunate that he happened to be executed, just hours ago, isn't it?" he asked, his smile widening.

Gwendolyn felt her throat go dry at her brother's words. Was it true? Or was he bluffing? She didn't know what to believe anymore.

"You are a liar," she said.

This time, he outright laughed.

"I might be. But I'm a much better liar than anyone else. I knew all about your pathetic little plot, all along. You vastly underestimated me. You always have. I have spies everywhere. I tracked everything you've done, every step of the way. I took action when the time was right. Your sole witness is dead, I'm afraid—and your murder weapon is quite useless without him. As for our dear brother, Godfrey—well, there's a reason he couldn't meet you here today."

Gwen's eyes opened wide in surprise, as she felt that Gareth was telling the truth.

"What do you mean?" she asked, tentatively.

"I'm afraid he had a bad drink last night at the tavern. I'm afraid someone might have poisoned it. He is deathly ill as we speak. In fact, I'm pretty sure he's dead already."

Gwen felt overcome with panic. Gareth laughed heartily.

"So you see, my dear, it is just you. There is no Godfrey. No Firth. No witness. Just you and your pathetic dagger, which proves nothing."

Gareth sighed.

"As for your lover, Thor," he continued, "I'm afraid his time has come, too. You see, this McCloud raid, which I tolerated for a reason, is a trap. Your lover is walking right into it. I've paid off men to isolate him, when the time is right. He will be ambushed, and will be quite alone, I assure you. He will be slaughtered by this day's end, and he will join Firth and Godfrey in heaven—or is it hell?"

Gareth laughed heartily, and she could see how maniacal he was. He looked possessed.

"I hope your soul rots in hell," she spat, seething with fury.

"It already is, my sister. And there is nothing left you can do touch me. But there is quite a deal still that I can do to touch you. Come tomorrow, you will be out of my hair, too. *Primos Livarius Stantos*," he said. "Do you know what that means?"

She stared at him, her heart cold, wondering what hideous plan he had devised.

"It is the legal term for a king's right to arrange a marriage."

He nodded and smiled.

"Very good. You always were the learned one. Far more learned than me. But that doesn't matter now. Because I've invoked it—I've invoked my right to force you into marriage. I have found a common man, a savage, a Nevarun soldier, the crudest province in the southern reaches of the Ring. They are already sending a contingent of men to fetch their bride. So pack your bags. You are chattel now. And you will never see my face again."

Gareth laughed hysterically, delighted with himself, and Gwen felt her heart tearing to pieces. She didn't want to believe any of it. Was he just playing with her mind?

She couldn't stand to be in front of him for another second. Gwen turned and fled the chamber, running down the corridor, up the spiral staircase, higher and higher, until she reached the parapets.

She ran to the far side, leaned over the edge and looked down over the town square. She had to see if it was true, if Firth was really executed, if everything he said had been a lie.

Gwen reached the edge and looked over, and as she did, her blood ran cold. She clutched her chest, gasping for air.

There, hanging by his neck from a rope, in the center of the square, was Firth. His body dangled, swayed in the wind, and a growing crowd gawked around it.

It was true. It was all true.

Gwen turned and ran to the other end of the parapets, looking East, searching desperately for Thor and the Legion. She spotted them on the horizon, hundreds of them, all on horseback, a great army, kicking up dust. The cloud was growing higher and higher, and she could see Thor among them, galloping with the others, so desperate to earn his glory. She thought of Gareth's words, of Thor being sent into a trap, sent to be ambushed. And as she watched him gallop away, she knew there was nothing she could do about it.

"NO!"

She screamed out to the heavens, sinking to her knees, wailing, pounding the stone, wishing it were anybody else, anything else. She couldn't imagine the thought of it. Gareth could kill her, could sell her away, could destroy everything in her life—but she could not imagine the thought of Thor being harmed.

"THOR!" she screamed.

She wished that he could hear her, that he could somehow turn, on the horizon, and return to her.

But her cry was picked up by the wind, carried away, and soon it vanished into nothing.

COMING SOON….
Book #4 in the Sorcerer's Ring

About Morgan Rice

Morgan Rice is the #1 Bestselling author of THE VAMPIRE JOURNALS, a young adult series comprising eight books, which has been translated into six languages.

Morgan is also author of the #1 Bestselling THE VAMPIRE LEGACY, a young adult series comprising two books and counting.

Morgan is also author of the #1 Bestselling ARENA ONE and ARENA TWO, the first two books in THE SURVIVAL TRILOGY, a post-apocalyptic action thriller set in the future.

Morgan loves to hear from you, so please feel free to visit www.morganricebooks.com to stay in touch.

Books by Morgan Rice

THE SURVIVAL TRILOGY
ARENA ONE (BOOK #1)
ARENA TWO (BOOK #2)

the Vampire Legacy
resurrected (book #1)
craved (book #2)

the Vampire Journals
turned (book #1)
loved (book #2)
betrayed (book #3)
destined (book #4)
desired (book #5)
betrothed (book #6)
vowed (book #7)
found (book #8)

5

CPSIA information can be obtained at www.ICGtesting.com
Printed in the USA
LVOW131320240613

339971LV00001B/7/P

9 781939 416094